SARATOGA STRONGBOX

BOOKS BY STEPHEN DOBYNS

SARATOGA STRONGBOX

■ A CHARLIE BRADSHAW MYSTERY ■

STEPHEN DOBYNS

VIKING

VIKING
Published by the Penguin Group
Penguin Putnam Inc., 375 Hudson Street,
New York, New York 10014, U.S.A.
Penguin Books Ltd, 27 Wrights Lane,
London W8 5TZ, England
Penguin Books Australia Ltd, Ringwood,
Victoria, Australia
Penguin Books Canada Ltd, 10 Alcorn Avenue,
Toronto, Ontario, Canada M4V 3B2
Penguin Books (N.Z.) Ltd, 182–190 Wairau Road,
Auckland 10, New Zealand

Penguin Books Ltd, Registered Offices:
Harmondsworth, Middlesex, England

First published in 1998 by Viking Penguin,
a member of Penguin Putnam Inc.

1   3   5   7   9   10   8   6   4   2

PUBLISHER'S NOTE
This is a work of fiction. Names, characters, places,
and incidents either are the product of the author's
imagination or are used fictitiously, and any
resemblance to actual persons, living or dead, events,
or locales is entirely coincidental.

LIBRARY OF CONGRESS CATALOGING IN PUBLICATION DATA
Dobyns, Stephen, date.
Saratoga strongbox : a Charlie Bradshaw mystery /
Stephen Dobyns.
p.   cm.
ISBN 0-670-87692-5
I. Title.
PS3554.O2S269   1998
813'.54—dc21   98-2886

This book is printed on acid-free paper.

Printed in the United States of America
Set in Goudy
Designed by Ellen Cipriano

FOR MARY KARR

Such aggressively minor suffering
wins no handshakes, roses, accolades
and threatens to suck the soul out,

though in a small compartment in your skull
you hope for finer things.
At night you set aside your lists
and dime-sized aches to lift its lid
and find the simple room
in which everything you meant to speak
and shape and do is spoken,
formed and done. . . .

—FROM "AVERAGE TORTURE"

BY MARY KARR

SARATOGA STRONGBOX

■ ONE ■

I was dipping my bill into a Jack Daniel's Manhattan when old man Weber came into the bar at the Parting Glass and we made eye contact. Maybe there was a little click. I felt it and he must have felt it too because he gave a smile: not a smile of greeting and good cheer, but a little self-satisfied smile. I guess that smile should have tipped me, but to tell the truth I felt flattered to be noticed. Not only was I noticed, but the old guy gave his cane a little shake and made a beeline in my direction.

I had known Felix Weber for some years, but only by reputation. He was Saratoga Springs' money man. A bunch of fellows of my acquaintance liked to say he was the smartest guy they ever met, but maybe that was because he helped them add up bushels of frequent flyer miles. Because you couldn't work for Weber without covering a lot of space. He was the money man and you were the courier, which meant Travel with a capital T. That's one of the details about Saratoga Springs. It lies half way between New York and Montreal.

One time I remember hearing how old man Weber realized there was twenty-nine cents of silver in each Canadian quarter. He bought tons. Maybe it was only a single ton. He melted it down and sold the silver. That was how his mind worked: four cents' difference multiplied by five, ten, twenty thousand. He was an exaggerator. He schlepped gold, silver, even dollars from one country to another and with the two or three or four cents' difference, he made himself rich. The total cash involved could be enormous. And all those figures, all those big numbers—that was how I got sucked into it.

I have always been the pal of easy money. What some people call temptation, I call opportunity. In the old days, it knocked; these days, it sends a fax. But isn't it a lack, a vacancy, an economic deficiency, that leads one into temptation? One would like more than one has got. It isn't greediness; it's dream. And I have to say I don't think of myself as dishonest, by which I mean I'd never rob a bank if there was the slightest chance of getting caught. On the other hand when a scam gets proposed, I find myself thinking up a better scam. Maybe this is human nature or it's just an example of how one gets fucked up. Someone offers me a deal where I make two bucks on the dollar, and I begin to imagine something more advantageous. But let's get back to old man Weber.

By now he was standing next to me. "Victor," he said, "I see by the maraschino cherry that you're drinking a Manhattan. Let me buy you another."

You understand how it is when somebody who you don't think knows your name, turns out to know your name? To tell the truth, I prefer Vic, but who was I to quibble? Weber was a short little guy, about five foot four—skinny with a thin face and a bristly mop of white hair. He resembled a toothbrush in more ways than one, except that he always wore suits and ties. He began to struggle up onto the stool beside me. I took hold of his elbow to give him a little assist.

"Stiff in the joints," he said.

"Story of my life," I said, just to be friendly.

The waiter had already caught the drift of our conversation and he set down in front of me another Jack Daniel's Manhattan, and in front of Weber he set a glass of milk.

Weber lifted the milk and toasted me with it. "To me," he said, "the cow says it best."

I nodded solemnly. "I started on the white stuff." If Weber had wanted to drink tiger piss, I would have been equally cordial, because, after all, he was paying for the drinks. But mostly I was curious. As far as I could recall, Weber and I had never swapped a single syllable, yet here he was with something on his mind. And whatever it was—at least this was what I told myself—it had to be connected to hard cash. Money was the country of which Weber formed the little flag. He had no other interests, no other topics, no other loyalties. So I composed my face into a respectful expression and waited.

"So, Victor," he said, "how's every little thing?"

"The market's been treating me kindly again," I answered. I had had some rather desperate stock market troubles a while ago, but now, like that Greek guy with his boulder, I was creeping back up the hill. "Not that I wouldn't like to do better."

Weber sipped his milk. It and his hair were the same color, except maybe the hair was whiter. "There's never been a stack of bills that couldn't be made higher," he opined.

"God's truth," I told him. Now this was pleasant chat but I was getting impatient for him to pare away the rye and get to the pastrami. Like just how many big bucks did he mean to toss in my direction?

"You got an automobile?" he asked.

"A Mercedes," I said.

"I like a man who drives a Mercedes."

"It's not new," I told him.

"The age isn't important. It's the spirit of the thing."

Actually it was twenty years old, had some rust and was painted an odd mustard color, but I understood what Weber was saying. "You feel it the moment you turn the key," I said.

He sipped some more milk, which gave him a little white mustache. "I'd heard you were driving a Yugo," he told me.

I assumed a humble expression. "It seemed politically correct for me to drive a Yugo for a while, but fortunately it passed away." I didn't know how much he knew about my problems but for some months I had a bunch of lawyers after me and the Yugo was meant to show that I was dead broke. Sad to say it didn't work.

"Then I heard you had a big new van."

"A passing fancy. It made me realize I'm a Mercedes kind of guy, not a van kind of guy." I didn't wish to say that the bank had relieved me of the van.

Old man Weber peered at me with a pair of light blue eyes. "How well do you know Montreal?" he asked.

I chuckled. "Montreal?" I said. "I know Montreal the way Batman knows guano." Actually, I had never been to Montreal.

"You ever drive up there?"

"The Mercedes loves long trips."

"I respect a man of the open road."

I smiled and nibbled my maraschino cherry. My wallet was in my back pocket and I was sitting on it. When Weber spoke, I could feel my wallet throb.

"You mind if we move over to a booth?" he asked.

So we moved to a booth. It was a Tuesday night in early March and only a dozen other people were in the bar: a couple of Skidmore students, a couple of drunks, a couple of red-nosed Irishmen researching their heritage by staring into pints of Guinness. I carried Weber's milk and he tottered after me, banging the chairs with his cane. I like old guys. Even though I'm sixty, or thereabouts, old guys always make me feel younger.

Once we were sitting easy, Weber twisted his face into an affable expression. "You think you could stand to make a little extra money?" His smile made him look like he had a chicken bone stuck in his throat.

"I never heard of anyone complain about having too much," I told him.

"I need someone to drive up to Montreal and pick up a suitcase."

So there it was. Opportunity, as they say, had whacked my gong. "The call of the road," I told him.

"It has to be done on Thursday evening," he said. "You pick up the suitcase at eight P.M. and you can be back here by eleven. How does two grand sound to you?"

Being an older guy, these figures were sometimes confusing. I mean, I had to tell myself that two thousand was no longer a fortune. Still, it was a pleasant hunk of change.

"Fan-tastic," I told him. "I feel tremendously honored by your confidence." But that wasn't quite true. Thursday night was March 10, a date that I might have easily forgotten had not the Queen of Softness threatened to carve it into my forehead with an Exacto knife. The Queen of Softness is my significant other, my half an orange, as the Ricans say. Her real name is Rosemary Larkin and she owns a lunch counter on the road to Schuylerville. I met her five years ago in the Parting Glass and it was love at first sight. She was so soft that her body seemed constructed from marshmallow and feathers. One sank into her like an alligator descends into the Okefenokee Swamp. The trouble was I had met her almost exactly five years ago and this Thursday was our anniversary and she had made big plans: dinner, dancing, soft lights and late-night games in the hot tub. I also knew that if I broke the date, she would feed me bit by bit into her Waring blender and serve me up as the blue plate special to the truck drivers and local farmers who came to taste her culinary wares. "Spicy," they would say. Nonetheless, I had no intention of kissing two thousand smackers good-bye.

I leaned over the table toward old man Weber. "It sounds like I'm your man."

The job was a piece of cake: a simple drive to Montreal, then I grab the suitcase and drive back to Saratoga. But though greedy, I wasn't completely foolhardy.

"So how come you want me to do this?" I asked. "I mean, you got to have other people you know better."

Weber rubbed his palms together and gave one of his bone-in-the-throat smiles. "I employ three couriers. One's down with the flu, one's in jail and one's on a trip to Miami. To tell the truth,

I didn't think of you until I saw you at the bar. Then a single word popped into my head: 'Mercedes.' You seemed a natural choice."

Did I realize that my vanity was being toyed with? Maybe I didn't care. I'd already decided I could farm this job out to somebody else for five hundred. Even a grand if I had to. I could turn it over to a confrere, keep my date with the Queen of Softness and be making money as I smooched.

"We got a deal," I said and I stuck out my hand.

We shook. Old man Weber's eyes glittered and my eyes must have glittered as well. We both trusted each other about as far as either of us could throw a Labrador retriever. Still, money spends sweetly no matter where it comes from. In this, sad to say, I turned out to be mistaken.

I got a pal named Charlie Bradshaw who's always short of cash. He is a private dick with a conscience, which is like a puritanical prostitute. If the Boy Scouts needed an in-house private cop, Charlie would be the guy for the job. I sometimes worry about his future. Like he's not much younger than I am and his health insurance is iffy, though he had been a Saratoga cop for twenty years and I expect he'll get a small pension. He does insurance work mostly, but he also goes after runaway teenagers and does surveillance. He is the kind of guy you tend to look across on your way to looking at something else. Maybe he is five nine, a little overweight, losing his hair, with round cheeks and a bump of a nose. As a fashion statement he resembles the Edsel. Rumpled seersucker is still important in his life. But if you look twice at his eyes you might rethink your hasty judgments. They are attentive: a light blue that rests on you like a bee rests on a flower. Very thoughtful. And he stands very still, almost as still as a brick. He stands still and watches and what he sees he feeds into his brain like feeding numbers into a computer. But most people don't notice his eyes or how he is standing, with the result that Charlie tends to be overlooked. You know how a heron stands in the water pretending to be a motionless bundle of sticks? That's how Charlie is. And that's how the little fishes get nabbed.

For twenty years Charlie has been living out at Saratoga Lake in a cottage: a gloomy place to my way of thinking with no company but loons and squirrels—nut cases one and all. He moved out there when he quit his job as a cop and divorced his wife. But, thank goodness, man cannot live on isolation alone and over the years Charlie has had several little romances. His most recent, now about six years old, is with a nurse named Janey Burris who has been after him to move into her house in town. Well, a few months ago Charlie took the big step, although he still has his cottage on the lake and he goes there at times to rest his ears because Janey has three teenage daughters who have a thousand qualities but on top of that they are loud and each has her own little stereo and several times when I've visited all three stereos were going like blazes and Charlie was sitting in the kitchen with cotton in his ears or wearing those noise suppressors that guys wear when they work with heavy machinery or jackhammers.

So it seemed to me that Charlie might jump at the chance to drive up to Montreal and make a few bucks. I would even let him use the Mercedes.

It was ten o'clock when Weber and I shook hands on the deal and I watched him gulp down the rest of his milk. Then he toddled to the door, gave me a wave and vanished into the night, presumably to count his lucre or however he passed his time during the wee hours. He had given me a five-hundred-dollar retainer and said he would tell me the details of my jaunt to Montreal at noon on Thursday. It was then I decided to drive over and talk to Charlie.

Janey Burris lived in a ramshackle three-story Victorian house over near the train station. She used to be married to a doofus who dumped her and ran off to Australia to wrestle with sheep and I guess Janey and him had originally bought the place as a love nest. But the trouble with a three-story Victorian love nest was it needed constant painting, plastering, plumbing and caretaking until Mr. Burris reached the decision that sheep were in fact preferable. Of course that would not have been my own preference, but I understand the reasoning by which he made his choice.

So now Charlie was doing the painting and plastering and, I have to say this in his favor, he was doing it with a good heart. He loved Janey and what he got from her was worth, for the time being, a little house work.

It was raining that night, a good March rain that would turn to snow before morning. There were still heaps of old snow along the curbs and they glistened in my headlights. Tree trunks gleamed. I parked in front and puddle-hopped to the front door. Inside, I found Charlie sitting at Janey's kitchen table wearing his noise suppressors. Janey must have been at work, jabbing people with needles and banging on babies' bottoms. Charlie didn't hear me knock. He was reading a book about Jesse James, his pal, and didn't care that the air was acoustically charged with Bob Marley, Pearl Jam and Blind Melon—all played loud. When he didn't hear me knock, I opened the door. When he didn't notice me, I tapped him on the shoulder.

He looked up with a smile. "Victor," he said.

"Vic," I answered.

"What?" Then he took off the noise suppressors.

"Why don't you tell them to turn it down?" I asked.

"If they're happy, I'm happy."

"Jesus, Charlie, don't go all nice on me."

By this time he was getting me a little whiskey—Jim Beam green—and pouring himself a splash as well. "So what brings you by so late?"

"You know old man Weber?"

"The money man?"

So I told him about seeing Weber in the Parting Glass and how he had hired me to pick up a suitcase in Montreal and how I wouldn't be able to do it. Of course, I didn't tell Charlie how much Weber had offered to pay me.

"How does a hundred bucks sound to you?" I said.

"What's wrong with his regular couriers?" asked Charlie.

"They're either busy or out of commission."

"But he must know dozens of other guys, why pick you?"

I rattled the ice cubs in my glass. "He likes the fact that I drive a Mercedes."

Charlie gave me a skeptical look. As I thought about it I had to admit that the whole business sounded a tad bogus. The music was still whanging away from the three stereos and I felt lightheaded.

"But the money's real," I said.

"How much did he offer you?"

"More than a hundred."

"How much more."

"Jesus, Charlie, I got to make a profit, don't I?"

"How much more?"

"He offered me two grand."

"And you offered me one hundred."

"I was willing to go up. You know how it goes. You haggle a little and I haggle a little."

We both had our elbows on the table and were leaning toward one another because of the noise. "I don't like this, Victor."

"All right, I'll give you five hundred."

"I don't mean the money. I just don't see why he'd hire you over someone else."

"He likes me. He thinks older men are more responsible."

Charlie didn't even bother to answer that.

"Okay, I'll give you a thousand. That's my last offer."

"Can't do it, Victor, even if I wanted to. Rosemary has invited Janey and me over to her place on Thursday for dinner. She said it was your anniversary or something."

So I was stuck. Beaten down by my own romance. But this defeat was only temporary, because I knew I could find somebody else to make the drive. There had to be lots of folks who were willing to pick up a few hundred extra.

"Just don't stay at Rosemary's too late," I said. "The Queen of Softness and me will have some serious smooching to do."

Charlie raised his eyebrows and had begun to edge his way toward a rudimentary wisecrack when there was a knocking on the kitchen door. Before anyone had a chance to say "Who is it?" pushy Eddie Gillespie pushed his way in. He wore a wet raincoat, which he stripped off as he entered. Underneath he had on white pajamas.

"You been selling Good Humor bars?" I asked.

Eddie looked indignant. "I just earned my black belt."

Charlie jumped up and began pumping his hand. "That's great, Eddie. It really is." He looked as happy as if Eddie had just won a lottery.

Eddie is in his mid-thirties but he likes to think himself a teenager, that is, irresponsible and irrepressible. He is an ex-crook—a car thief—who Charlie rescued long ago, and Eddie has hung around ever since, doing the odd job, sometimes working at Charlie's mother's hotel, a big place on Broadway called the Bentley that was only open during the summer. Eddie was a trim, not to say scrawny, youngster, with a careful mop of shiny black hair that was his major field of study. Like it wasn't as if the hair belonged to Eddie but Eddie belonged to the hair. Eddie was his hair's little servant. He flung it to the left to mean this, he flung it to the right to mean that. It wasn't a head of hair, it was a text. I mostly called him Doofus Gillespie, but not to his face.

"I been studying this karate stuff for fifteen years," said Eddie. "And now I got my black belt."

It seemed to me that if you took fifteen years to learn a subject, then you must be some kind of slow learner, but I'd had an idea and didn't wish to be provocative. "That's great, Eddie. This calls for celebration." I poured him some Jim Beam green.

Eddie took the glass and we clicked glasses just like the Three Musketeers. We smiled at one another. I gave Eddie a wink, the doofus: big, brave and a black belt.

"Say, Eddie," I began. "How'd you like to make an easy hundred bucks?"

"A hundred?" asked Eddie, becoming attentive.

"Hell," I said, "let's make it two hundred. Just how well do you know Montreal?"

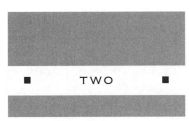

TWO

The good news was that Eddie promised to make the drive. The bad news was that he pushed me to a solid grand: a thousand smackers for a simple taxi job. Plus I had to let him use the Mercedes and fill it with gas before he left. But he also promised on his mother's grave not to drive over seventy miles per hour, whatever that was worth. Maybe he hated his mother. Now all that remained to be done was to find out where he was supposed to pick up the suitcase, then he would deliver it to me Thursday evening at Rosemary's and I would shoot it over to old man Weber. I hoped the Queen of Softness could do without my presence for at least half an hour, but when you are as much in love as she is, even a scant thirty minutes away from the sacred flesh is a misery. At least that was what I thought then.

But that same Tuesday night I had a little shock. Hey, who am I kidding, it was a big shock. It was a shock like Sing Sing used to give out shocks, like Alcatraz. I had promised Rosemary I would drop by her place around midnight for a few hugs, kisses, and maybe a tuna fish sandwich, but having finished with Charlie and Doofus Gillespie earlier than I anticipated, I got over to her place at shortly after eleven.

Her lunch counter was set off by itself ("Rosemary's: Family Eats Can't Be Beat") and behind it was the small ranch house that she called home. There were fields on three sides and across the road. A few scattered maples provided shade in the summer. Sort of a lonely place but during the day the Queen of Softness always drew a crowd. As I was driving out there, the rain changed to snow. I don't know about you, but I hate dirty snow, by which I mean snow that has been sitting around turning gray and collecting dog poop, and although I was getting pretty sick of winter, I was at least grateful that we were getting a new layer of white to cover up the dead stuff. Of course, the Mercedes doesn't mind snow. It would drive straight across the unplowed fields if I wanted it to.

As I was approaching the diner, I saw a car pull out from the side and head east toward Schuylerville. At first I wasn't sure that it had been at the diner or maybe it had only turned around. But when I pulled into the parking lot, I saw its tire tracks in the snow—only about half an inch at that point—and a bare place in front of Rosemary's little house where it had been parked. There were even footprints leading from Rosemary's front door to the car. These were a man's footprints, big Vibram soles.

I didn't think too much of this. Obviously, the Queen of Softness had had a visitor, but who was I to say she couldn't? I don't think of myself as a jealous guy, not even a suspicious guy, but I was mildly curious.

I knocked on the door, rang the bell and stamped the snow off my feet. Rosemary opened up. She is a big woman with platinum blond hair piled high on her head. All her features are oversized, which is how I like them. Like Rosemary is the enemy of subtlety and understatement. She was wearing a red silk dressing gown with an ermine collar and little gold slippers that looked a trifle tight on her pink feet.

"Oh, Victor," she said, as if she hadn't been expecting me. I entered and gave her a peck on the cheek. "Who was your visitor?" I asked.

"Visitor?"

"Yeah, I saw a car pulling away."

"Probably someone just turning around."

"But there are footprints."

"Oh, *that* person. Just someone asking for directions. She saw my light—"

"She?"

"She wasn't sure if this was the road to Schuylerville."

You know how it is when you decide not to ask any more questions because you are afraid to hear what you don't want to hear? I was ninety-nine percent positive that the footsteps had belonged to a man. And because of the bare spot where the car had been parked, it seemed obvious that the car had been there since before it started snowing, which meant at least half an hour. And, of course, the only footprints had been leading away from the house. Not to the house.

We were still standing by the door and Rosemary was giving me a jolly smile, but I saw some tension behind it. Believe me, I was thrown for a triple figure eight. It was half on my mind to tell her that she was fibbing to her sweetie, but then what? Do I stomp out? Do I throw a fit? On the other hand, it seemed clear that another man had been paying Rosemary a visit that she was covering up. This was not a happy discovery.

"Would you like a sandwich?" asked Rosemary. "I got some fresh turkey breast and honey mustard. How does that sound? You can eat it in the hot tub. You want a Heineken to go with it?"

I'm sure I was looking at her suspiciously, but slowly I let myself be coaxed back to a state of good cheer, though not entirely. We ate, we drank, we played in her hot tub, we made our celebration plans for our fifth anniversary on Thursday night, we went to bed. But as I was nodding off to sleep, I again saw those taillights pulling away from Rosemary's diner and I wondered if I would recognize them if I saw them again: one long horizontal bar of red light.

On Thursday morning I called old man Weber and he told me to come over to his house on Court Street about three blocks from the Museum of Racing. It was one of these Victorian affairs that often get turned into funeral homes. One hundred years ago, they were called cottages, that is, cottages for the rich and famous visiting from New York City for the Saratoga season: some horses, some roulette, some questionable water at the baths and carriage rides out to the lake: the pre-TV kind of life. The house had a wraparound porch, two turrets and a big stained glass window showing a lady in what looked like a nightgown descending a flight of stairs.

Weber let me in and we talked in the hall. If there was a Mrs. Weber, we weren't introduced, although I knew that Weber's son, Joey, sometimes lived with him, especially when he was broke. The hall had a mildew smell: the smell, I thought, of damp money. From a room nearby came the sound of several canaries singing their tiny hearts out. Weber was wearing a tan leisure suit and tan Italian moccasins. His stiff white hair was neatly combed so it stood up straight. I had a passing desire to pick him up and clean the walls with him. He could have done an infomercial for Fuller Brush.

Weber handed me a scrap of cardboard. "This is a claim check. Hand it to the concierge at the Hotel du Parc at eight o'clock this evening and he will give you a suitcase. Make sure it is exactly at eight o'clock. Then deliver the suitcase to me at eleven sharp and I will give you the other fifteen hundred. If by any chance you have trouble, do not contact the police."

My antennae began to flutter. "You expecting trouble?"

"Of course not, but there's always a possibility. After all, there's a lot of money involved. But to contact the police would make it worse."

"Gotcha," I said. "What if I get searched at the border?"

"That's very unlikely, but if a customs officer opens the suitcase, he will only find clothes."

"A false bottom?" I asked.

Weber gave me a wink. "Just like Mae West."

So early that afternoon I had Eddie Gillespie drop by my apartment at the Algonquin on Broadway.

"A piece of cake," I said, giving him the claim check. "Just make sure you pick up the bag at exactly eight o'clock."

"Why eight o'clock?" asked Eddie, who always has a problem with everything.

"Because that's when it's going to be there," I said.

Eddie was wearing a black pinstripe suit, a black silk shirt and a white tie. And he was chewing gum. Even when standing still, Eddie's black hair seemed to undulate.

"You been watching old George Raft movies?" I asked.

He was surprised. "How could you tell?"

"Just make sure that you bring the suitcase out to Rosemary's no later than ten thirty."

"I want half the money before I go," said Eddie. "It's my kid's birthday tomorrow. She's turning four."

Eddie has a little brat by name of Angelina who seems to be able to wear nothing but pink dresses. Eddie's wife Irene said she was grooming her for Hollywood. To my mind Angelina was plump enough that if you put a red dress on her she could pass for a fire hydrant, but I kept my lip buttoned.

"That's swell, Eddie," I said. "Every kid should have a birthday once in a while. You going to give her five hundred smackers?"

"I'd like to buy her a little dress up in Montreal," said Eddie, shoving a hand through his black hair so it rose up like a black Niagara Falls. "Something French."

I was scheduled to show up at Rosemary's at six o'clock. Charlie and Janey Burris were scheduled to arrive at seven. I had purchased the Queen of Softness some very sexy underwear at a mall down in Colonie, north of Albany, and I was hoping to see her try it out: feathers and supplemental openings.

Well, that's not quite true. I didn't buy the stuff myself; I hired a young lady to buy it. The Queen of Softness is almost exactly my size and, unfortunately, whenever I buy her intimate garments, the salesclerk thinks I am buying them for myself; that is, I intend to wear them myself. I don't know if you have ever tried to tell a cute salesclerk that you are not buying this extra-extra-large sequined bra and panties for yourself, but if you do then probably, like me, you will not be believed. The last time I tried to make such a purchase, a girl young enough to be my granddaughter took me aside and asked if I didn't want to go someplace private and slip them on. I don't embarrass easy and maybe I wasn't embarrassed then, but ever since I have employed a young lady to do my intimate shopping.

So I had these nicely gift-wrapped items, plus a box of Godiva chocolates and a couple of bottles of wine, but what I was really tempted to do was to show up an hour earlier to see if I could catch Rosemary with somebody: the mysterious stranger. And it occurred to me, was this any way to celebrate our fifth anniversary? But ever since Tuesday night, I had been brooding about the car I'd seen pulling away from the diner, and whenever I saw a car with a long horizontal bar of taillights, I would give the driver a hawklike look. The thought that another mule had been banging in my stall didn't sit comfy with me.

Anyway, I got to her place at six when it was just getting dark and Rosemary's baby blue Crown Victoria was the only car in evidence. She was still getting dressed and had on her red silk dressing gown. I gave her the presents and Godiva chocolates, all nicely wrapped. There was also a little bracelet with gold hearts on it.

"For me?" she said and she gave me a peck on the cheek that nearly knocked me off the front step.

I followed her inside. There were balloons and flowers everywhere. Some kind of cha-cha music was playing on the stereo. The Queen of Softness has several white Angora cats and they were lounging on the furniture like sex toys.

Rosemary gave me a close look. "Why so glum, chum?"

I hadn't thought it showed. "Ingrown toenail," I told her.

"I can take care of that. Just cut a little *V* in the nail. Here, let me do it. Which foot?"

She made a beeline for my shoes and I stepped back. "It's not an actual ingrown toenail. I just got the spiritual version of an in-grown toenail. I got an ingrown toenail in my soul."

Rosemary gave me a queer look, then shrugged. "You make yourself a drink and I'll finish getting dressed." I made myself a Jack Daniel's Manhattan with two mara-schino cherries. A roast was sizzling in the oven, potatoes were simmering on the stove, champagne was chilling in the fridge. Eddie Gillespie was about to pick up the Montreal strongbox and make me a thousand smackers. Why couldn't I be happy? And again I saw the car pulling away from Rosemary's diner.

I drank my drink and made another. Rosemary was whistling as she got dressed: "There Ain't Nothin' Like a Dame." Her place is small but it's open with the living room, kitchen and dining room separated by a couple of counters. The sofas are covered with fake animal fur: tigers and leopards. There are fake fur rugs on the floor: polar bears and zebras. On the walls are paintings of animals on black velvet: a lion dragging down a gazelle, a cheetah nabbing an antelope, a wolf looking up from a bloodied rabbit. Sometimes Rosemary puts wild animal roars on the stereo—lions or wolves—and the whole place gets very weird. Looking at the gazelle, ante-lope and rabbit that were becoming dinner for something bigger and furrier, I felt a moment of identification. Isn't this a truism? Can't anybody become dinner for somebody else? No matter how smart we think we are, we are basically no more than lunch, whether it be for ants, maggots or something bigger. Hadn't the roast sizzling in the oven once glanced at its reflection in a glisten-ing pool and mooed, "Hey, I'm a handsome hunk of beef!" What with thoughts like this I worked my way to my third Manhattan.

Charlie and Janey Burris showed up at seven. Charlie always likes arriving on the dot. He thinks lateness is a moral failing. Rosemary was wearing a lilac-colored gown that showed a lot of bosom crisscrossed with strings of lapis.

"Tell Victor some jokes," she said. "He's feeling low."

"I'm fine," I said. In one hour Eddie would be picking up the suitcase in Montreal.

Charlie wore a blue blazer and gray slacks. His tie looked like it had spent its first twenty years serving as the finish line for the Boston Marathon. His hair was slicked down and age had finally freed him of his cowlick, meaning it had fallen out. "You do look a little somber," he said.

"Maybe we should tickle him," said Janey. She wiggled her fingers at me. She is a tidy number who does aerobics and runs. Her short black hair is getting some gray. She was wearing a tight purple-and-yellow dress that showed her lines. She's cute but a little scrawny to my taste: a trifle too nouvelle cuisine.

"I'm really okay," I said. "Let's party."

I got to say I worked hard. I told some jokes. I put the lampshade on my head. I had Rosemary open her packages of sexy underwear and Charlie blushed.

"Why don't you ever buy me something like that?" Janey asked him. Charlie's idea of pajamas is flannel. He even used to wear a nightcap until Janey broke him of it.

Janey opened the champagne and the cork shot across the room. One of the Angora cats chased it, then began batting it around. "It's nice to be away from the girls," Janey said. "They have several boyfriends and the house has a musky smell."

"Aren't you afraid of leaving them on their own with those boys?" asked Rosemary.

"They guard each other," said Janey. "So when one is searching for privacy, the other two keep interrupting. If they ever join forces, I'll be a grandmother for sure."

It was all very pleasant. Now and then I would check my watch and tell myself that Eddie was now driving back to Saratoga or that he was in the last one hundred miles.

At one point when Charlie and I were clearing the table, he said to me, "I asked around about Weber's usual couriers. Nobody's sick, nobody's in jail."

"Meaning he never needed me to do the run?"

"That's right."

"You think Eddie's all right?"

"I hope so."

We worried a little. I mean, Eddie's a jerk, but I would hate to see anything happen to him. I kept looking at my watch and thinking of his little girl: Angelina, all dressed in pink. Eddie might be a lousy dad but he was the only dad she had. However, the worrying turned out to be unnecessary. At ten fifteen we heard a car in front followed shortly afterward by Eddie's jivey knock on the front door.

"A piece of cake," he said as he handed me the suitcase.

"Is the Mercedes all right?" I asked.

"No problem. You know that old crate can still do one hundred and ten? Makes you appreciate European craftsmanship."

In a couple of minutes, I left them eating chocolate mousse and drinking champagne as I drove over to old man Weber's with the suitcase.

I had to ring the bell about five minutes before he came to the door. He looked at me uncertainly.

"You got it?" he asked.

"It's right here in my hand."

He took the suitcase, put it on the hall table and opened it up. I saw a bunch of folded shirts. Weber tossed them on the floor and dug down to the false bottom. He pulled it up and I could see a happy bunch of greenbacks lying side by side.

"You got the money?" he said.

I wondered if he was getting a little senile. He wore a maroon paisley robe and had his slippers on. Maybe he had been sleeping and his brain was still iffy.

"Looks like money to me," I said.

"And you had no problems?"

"A piece of cake."

"You really had no problems?" The expression on his face indicated worry and somehow I didn't think he had been worried about me.

"That's what I said, didn't I. Do I get my fifteen hundred smackers now?"

He looked at me, opened his mouth to speak, then just shook his head and began to count out the money.

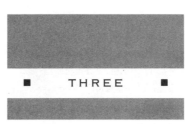

■ THREE ■

Well, this made me curious. Why should old man Weber be surprised that I showed up with the money? I brooded about this as I drove back to Rosemary's: the pros and cons, the ups and downs. Eddie was still there, slurping champagne and stuffing his face with chocolate mousse. Now and then he would pause to ruffle his hair. Actually, he seemed to be scratching it more than tossing it. Charlie was yawning—he likes to go to bed early—and Rosemary was telling Janey something about mascara and how it could change her life.

"So tell me, Eddie," I said, after I had taken off my coat and poured myself a little Jack, "you really had no problems up in Montreal?"

"A piece of cake," Eddie repeated with his mouth full of chocolate mousse. But he said it, I thought, without one hundred percent belief and I saw Charlie click open his eyes and look at him. Eddie swallowed, then dabbed his lips with a napkin.

"Eddie," I said, "if nothing really happened, how come you're looking funny?"

"Funny?" asked Eddie. His face began to go red.

"Funny as if you were lying," said Charlie.

"Oh, Eddie," said Janey Burris, disappointed.

By this point Eddie had everyone's attention. "Jesus," he said. "You people are supposed to be my friends."

"We are your friends," said Charlie, soothingly. "That's why we like you to tell the truth."

"So what happened?" I asked.

Eddie stared down at his pointed George Raft shoes. "You'll yell at me."

"No one will yell at you," said Charlie.

I wasn't ready to promise that myself. I wanted to hear what he had done before I decided whether to yell or not. But I kept my mouth shut.

Eddie poured himself some more champagne. He stood near the counter separating the kitchen from the living room and he kept tossing his hair as if it helped him to think. "Well, I drove up there like I said I would," he began. "And I went into the hotel and gave the claim check to the porter, what they call a concierge up there." Eddie pronounced it "con-sarge." "And the concierge gave me the suitcase. That's all there was to it."

"Then what happened?" asked Charlie.

Eddie gnawed a little on his lower lip, then picked an invisible speck off his white silk tie. "I'd parked the Mercedes around back near a service entrance. The hotel was a pricey place full of rich people talking French. I went out the side door. It was dark but there were some streetlights and people were milling around. I was just unlocking the door of the Mercedes, when it happened."

We waited.

"Aren't you going to ask me what happened?" asked Eddie.

"What happened?" said Charlie.

"Someone stuck a gun in my back," said Eddie. Then he let out a deep breath and shook his head.

We were silent a moment, then Rosemary asked, "Were you scared?"

Eddie looked embarrassed and shook his head again.

"Not even a little frightened?" asked Janey.

Eddie shook his head a third time, jostling the interior cobwebs most likely. "You see, I've been waiting years for this. Fifteen years I've been studying karate and I've never got the chance to use it. Sure, maybe in bars, some guy might get rude but the moment I go into my crouch and show him my hands he gets all apologetic. So here is this guy shoving a gun in my back, actually touching me with the cold steel barrel. It felt great."

" 'Great,' " said Charlie as if to make sure he had heard correctly. "As in 'feels good.' "

"That's right, but you see it was also wrong. That gun barrel was the very voice of temptation. In karate you study the power so you won't have to use it. You're trying to raise yourself above the whole idea of power. When this guy stuck the gun in my back, I should have raised myself above the situation. I mean, mentally raised myself. I should have opened my mind to pure thoughts. Instead, I felt glad. I felt eager to hurt him."

"And did you?" I asked.

Eddie put his hands over his eyes and nodded.

"What happened?" asked Charlie. We had moved closer to Eddie and were standing in a semicircle around him. His butt was pressed up against the kitchen counter.

"He had the gun pressed to my back and told me to give him the suitcase. He muttered it and at first I wasn't sure what he was talking about. But once I realized what was going on I gave him a little side arm block, which paralyzed his hand. After that I snapped his wrist and kicked his feet out from under him. I feel so ashamed." Eddie lowered his head.

"But you liked it," I suggested.

"I loved it," said Eddie.

"Then what happened?" asked Charlie.

Eddie squinched shut his eyes. "I kicked him."

"Once?" asked Janey.

"Twice," said Eddie.

"Only twice?" asked Charlie.

"Maybe three times."

"And how did it make you feel?" asked Janey.

"Fantastic," said Eddie. "I mean, I'd been studying absolutely forever for a moment like this. I didn't just kick him, I kicked him in special places that would specially disable him. But I failed, I lost control. I let my pleasure center take over. I could have easily disarmed him without hurting him, but I found I wanted to hurt him. I wanted to give him pain." Eddie drank some more champagne, then wiped his mouth on the back of his hand. "I feel awful."

"But you got the suitcase," I said, trying to look at the bright side.

"I would have gotten the suitcase anyway. I didn't have to whomp the guy and I didn't have to have such a good time doing it. I've let down my teacher, my entire class. Driving back down, I looked in the rearview mirror and said, 'Fifteen years shot to hell.' I'm sure I'll be punished for this. The Buddha or God or somebody, he'll bust my ass."

Charlie and Janey tried to comfort him. Rosemary gave him more champagne. I reminded myself that I didn't call him Doofus Gillespie for nothing. And I suggested that since he had messed up he wouldn't be wanting the other five hundred bucks, but he did. He counted out the bills and added them to the five hundred already in his possession but it didn't cheer him in the least. He drank more champagne and looked pathetic. Hell, he would have been happy drinking Schlitz. A few minutes later he decided to slouch back to Ballston Spa, where he lived with his wife and kid: the darling Angelina. Ten minutes after that Charlie and Janey left as well.

When we were alone, I poured the Queen of Softness another glass of champagne. All she knew was that Eddie had an errand in Montreal. I had told her nothing about old man Weber, mostly because she is a law-abiding sort and when she feels that I am working at the cutting edge of the law, she tends to fret.

I wasn't exactly sure what law Eddie had broken, but I should think that sneaking a suitcase of money across the border would make any number of police officer types raise their eyebrows. The Queen of Softness was in the dark and I saw no reason to offer her a flashlight. The main reason was my own uncertainty. It seemed obvious that old man Weber had expected trouble and it was only Doofus Gillespie's expertise with the karate chop that had enabled him to come home with the swag. But what if I had gone to Montreal instead of Eddie? The only chops I knew were pork, lamb and veal—meaning I would have been robbed for certain.

This made me wonder about Weber's other couriers, who he had claimed were indisposed, but who Charlie said were the picture of health and as free as the proverbial birds. And this made me think that Weber had wanted me—I mean me in particular—to go up to Montreal because he saw me as an aging old fart of sixty or thereabouts whose only weight training consisted of bending his elbow at the bar and letting out his belt every time he knocked back another hot fudge sundae. This did not make me happy. It suggested that Weber was making a patsy out of me. It suggested that he saw me as no Charlie Atlas or that guy Schwarzenegger who wrestles football teams for lunch.

But I also thought, Hey, you've made a thousand smackers, forget about the stuff you don't understand. Sad to say, I didn't listen. It seemed where I'd made a thousand smackers, I could make another thousand or two or three thousand. Although I wasn't sure how to do it, I still hoped to turn this business to greater profit.

But this was no time to brood about such matters. The Queen of Softness and I were alone and she had turned up the tango music. The lights were dimmed, the champagne cold, the music hot and my temperature rising. Rosemary threw off her feather boa. I put my hand around her waist and we swirled across the floor to the rhythms of "Hernando's Hideaway." My nose was pressed into the perfume of her platinum blond hair and I felt like a honeybee plunging its proboscis into the depths of an eager orchid. Time, as they say, whisked past.

But the next morning as I lay in my own bed and listened to Moshe III, my one-eyed cat, clumping around the apartment in search of snacks, I turned my mind again to old man Weber. Who was this guy that Eddie had whacked and how bad had he been hurt?

Eddie Gillespie had a job for the city driving a snowplow, which meant, as far as I could see, that the city paid him to uproot parking meters, because Eddie had destroyed a bundle. After I'd finished my morning coffee, I called the city garage to see if I could track him down. I was told that Eddie had called in sick and was still at home. So I called Eddie at home.

"I don't want to talk about it," said Eddie.

"Jesus, Eddie, I only want to know how badly you hurt the guy."

"I said, I don't want to talk about it." Eddie's voice sounded muffled, as if he was talking through a washcloth.

"You think you broke anything besides his wrist?"

"Vic, can't you understand? I don't want to talk about it. I did a bad thing and now I'm being punished."

"Just how are you being punished, Eddie?"

"I itch."

"Itch?"

"That's what I said, isn't it? I itch."

Eddie hung up. I stared at the phone and wondered if Charlie had really thought he was improving the quality of life by keeping Doofus Gillespie out of jail twenty years ago and maybe people like Doofus Gillespie were born to be in jail. Maybe it was their karma. Maybe they'd only be happy in jail.

Anyway I decided to pay a visit to Charlie.

It was a sunny morning but cold. More snow had fallen in the night—about five inches—and salesclerks were shoveling the sidewalks in front of their stores. I walked past police headquarters, crossed against the light at Lake Avenue and paused in front of Bookworks to scope out the headlines in the *Times* (Iraq was complaining again and things were tense in Taiwan). The T-shirt shops had packed away their Saratoga T-shirts till summer. There was nothing to show that horses were more important here than anyplace else on the planet, although the harness track was running. Whenever it wasn't, then the place was open for off-track betting. It was one of those March mornings when spring doesn't seem too far away and the birds are making flirtatious calls to one another. And it was Friday: the weekend and its pleasures lay ahead. Drivers didn't look so discouraged and some of the folks on the sidewalk even had a smile. Me, I said hello to the ladies and nodded to the men. Mr. Affable, that's what I call myself.

Charlie has an office on the second floor of a building on Phila Street right over a used bookstore. He has got a little anteroom with some old magazines and moribund chairs, and his office is on the other side of a frosted glass partition. I rapped on the glass and entered. Charlie was sitting at the desk with his sleeves rolled up. Around him were dozens of little pieces of paper and he looked up from them dolefully.

"Taxes," he said.

"Oklahoma," I answered.

His office was sparse: a desk and chair, a file cabinet, a safe and two visitor chairs. On the wall behind the desk was a big framed photograph of Jesse James. Charlie liked Jesse James for a number of reasons and today he liked him because Jesse never paid taxes. Tomorrow he might like Jesse because Jesse never watched his cholesterol. The day after it might be because Jesse was never polite to folks he didn't feel like being polite to. Everyday there was something new in Jesse's favor, but most of them were negatives; that is, stuff that Jesse didn't do or stuff that he didn't like or didn't put up with. For Charlie, this was all in Jesse's favor. For me, it explained why Jesse got a bullet in his head at the age of thirty-five. Jesse was many things, I'd tell Charlie, but he wasn't circumspect and he had no tact. Reckless actions lead to reckless consequences.

"Don't you do your taxes?" asked Charlie after I sat down.

The room was cool but he was in his shirtsleeves and had beads of sweat on his brow.

"I get someone to do them for me."

"But what about the receipts?"

"I'm a great guesstimator."

"Do you mean you lie?"

"I just let my creative juices flow."

We chatted like this for a few minutes, but I could see it only made Charlie more unhappy and depressed, so I switched the subject to old man Weber and the topic of my visit.

"As close as I can figure it," I told Charlie, "Weber picked me because he knew I would get robbed and he wanted someone who would get robbed easily."

"You mean he thought you'd be a pushover."

"You bet."

Charlie was looking at me with a half-smile. "But he didn't realize you were devious."

"Right again."

"Do you know anything about this money you were supposed to pick up?"

"Nothing."

Charlie pinched the bridge of his nose a couple of times and sniffed. "Maybe Weber was trying to rob himself. Maybe he was letting someone else rob him on purpose. Maybe it was a dummy suitcase with dummy money: a real bill on a stack of paper. Maybe all this has something to do with you personally. Maybe Weber was testing you to see if he could trust you with something else. Maybe one of a dozen other reasons." Charlie raised his fingers and thumbs with his various suggestions.

"Why would he rob himself?"

Charlie began raising his fingers again, like he is a man with a passion for counting. "Maybe to keep from paying somebody else. Maybe to collect some kind of insurance. Maybe to rob a partner. Again, there are lots of maybes."

"So what do you think I should do?"

"Nothing. You got your money. Just count yourself lucky and forget it."

"Maybe there is more money to be had," I suggested.

Charlie sucked his teeth, then shoved his tongue under his

upper lip to check the results. "What happens when you let your appetite make the decisions in your life?"

"You tell me," I said, already knowing the answer.

"You get in trouble."

"Always?"

"Ninety percent of the time."

It was on the tip of my tongue to ask Charlie what I should do if old man Weber called me again, but I decided to keep that question to myself. I'd made a thousand bucks doing nothing. Wasn't that the American dream? The stiller I stood, the richer I would get. At most I might give old man Weber a little nudge just to remind him of my presence.

After I left Charlie, I spent the rest of the morning studying my investments. There were fewer than I would have liked. I had hoped they would grow but they appeared to be lying fallow. Maybe that was one of the reasons that later in the afternoon, I gave Weber a call.

"What's on your mind, Plotz?" he asked, in a way that was a shade less than friendly.

"I'm calling to say I'm still around if you need me."

He made a noise that might have been laughter or might have been phlegm. "You think I thought you dropped dead?"

"I'm just reminding you of my availability in case there's anything you might want picked up someplace," I said.

"Believe me, Plotz," he said, "I won't forget you."

"I like to be called Vic," I said.

"Noted," he said.

That night I had made no plans to see the Queen of Softness. After our excesses of the previous night, I felt it best to let her rest and unwind for at least twenty-four hours to give her a chance to recuperate. Otherwise, I had arranged for some guys to play cards in my apartment and, although I would not be playing myself, I supplied the sandwiches, the drinks and the cards. For this I received a portion of the pot. It was another way of earning money without actually doing anything. Possibly I was destined on this earth to be no more than a paperweight. But I kept thinking about the car I'd seen pulling away from Rosemary's house on Tuesday night, so twice I left the game and drove by her lunch counter. My fears were groundless. Her car was there and no one else's: just the way I like it. I began to think that her story about the car had been correct: someone had been asking for directions. Perhaps I had misjudged her.

On Saturday I had promised to take the Queen of Softness out to dinner: steaks at the Firehouse. I said I would pick her up at seven but I showed up at six just to see what was to be seen. Rosemary was alone, scrubbing behind her ears in anticipation of my arrival. She was surprised to see me so soon but was glad nonetheless. I got a hug and a couple of kisses. After dinner we returned to her house to play in her hot tub for several hours till my skin was as wrinkled as Methuselah's scrotum.

On Sunday evening, I told Rosemary I had to go down to Albany. It was a lie. I didn't have to go anyplace. In the late afternoon, I called her several times and her phone was busy. It irked me. I mean, who else did she have to talk to except me? Then I called Charlie over at Janey Burris's. He was taking a nap but I got Janey to wake him.

"Hey, Charlie," I asked, "how difficult is it to put a tap on someone's phone? I want to hire you to do it."

He made a grumbling noise. "Legally or illegally?"

"Illegally."

"Forget it, Victor, we'd wind up in jail."

"Sometimes jail is worth it," I said. "Don't you need the money?"

"Sometimes the money's not worth it."

We talked about this for a while but the upshot was that he refused to help. Some friend, right?

Around six thirty I drove out to Rosemary's, not to stop but to drive by and take a peek at the landscape. Her car wasn't there but another car was: a dark late-model Dodge. Let me say that the taillights made a long horizontal bar. I wasn't going to stop but I couldn't help myself The lights were off in the house. I knocked on the door but there was no answer. I checked over the

Dodge pretty carefully. It was locked. In the backseat was a base-ball mitt, a Wilson. I got chills. It seemed that Rosemary was see-ing a sportsman. I also decided they had gone into Saratoga for dinner and that they had taken Rosemary's car. So I drove back to Saratoga to check the restaurants.

Jealousy—it's a burning in the gut. There was a ferocious sense of disbelief coupled with the conviction of betrayal. I checked fif-teen restaurants going faster and faster. The last four or five I prac-tically stiff-armed the maître d' as I shoved my way through the smoking and nonsmoking sections. I began to imagine the type of guy Rosemary had gone out with: scrawny like Valentino and wear-ing a dark sharkskin suit and lots of Vitalis.

Shortly after ten o'clock I went back to my apartment for my baseball bat: a Louisville slugger that I kept for nonathletic pur-poses. I figured even if I couldn't find Rosemary and her pal, I could at least drive out to her place and smash his windshield. Maybe the headlights as well. The symmetry of this pleased me. Didn't he have a baseball mitt in his backseat?

My answering machine was flashing and I figured it was Rosemary calling to apologize. It wasn't. It wasn't even Charlie Bradshaw.

"Vic," came the voice, "this is Felix Weber. I would like to ex-change a few words with you. I can make it worth your while. Per-haps we can meet at ten thirty this evening at the Parting Glass."

My watch said ten twenty-five. I thought for a nanosecond: Weber on one side, Rosemary on the other. Then I headed for the door. There is nothing like the chance of money to make one forget one's emotional problems. What was jealousy and betrayal when held up against the possibility of making another thousand smackers by doing positively nothing? Absolutely zip. Surely, it was on principles such as these that America was made.

■ FOUR ■

Old man Weber was at the bar nursing a big glass of cow juice when I hurried into the Parting Glass and waved hello. From the back room came the tweedle of Irish pipes and I could see from Weber's expression—maybe it was the way his false teeth were clenched—that for him the expression "Irish music" was oxymoronic. I thought he would be irritated at my tardiness, but when he saw me, his expression turned to relief and his wrinkles began to curve upward instead of down.

"Vic," he said.

"The very same," I told him as I climbed onto the next stool.

Jimmy the bartender began preparing a Jack Daniel's Manhattan with two maraschino cherries.

"Thank you for being so prompt," said Weber.

"My mother always told me to be on time," I explained.

"I like a fellow versed in the old values," said Weber. He licked the mustache of milk from his upper lip. He was looking dapper in a dark suit and tie. On his feet were a pair of black rubber galoshes.

"Most likely I would have entered the church," I told him, "were it not for a keen interest in the other sex."

"True, all too true," said Weber.

I waited. Jimmy plunked down the Manhattan in front of me and gave me a wink. I stuck my nose in the glass. Slowly, feelings of humanity and goodness began to reenter my heart.

Weber sipped his milk, then patted his lips with the back of his hand. His stiff white hair was brushed up and it appeared he had had a trim since I had seen him last. Each hair looked like a little albino soldier standing at attention.

"How would you like to make another little drive?" he asked.

"To Montreal?"

He glanced around to see if we could be overheard. Nobody was sitting nearby and the pipes were still tweedling away in the other room. "But to another hotel," he said at last.

I partook of my drink and tried to look philosophical. "I would certainly hate to have any trouble."

"A piece of cake."

"That's what you said last time."

"And wasn't it?" he asked, raising his eyebrows at me.

Now of course I had not told Weber that Eddie Gillespie had driven up to Montreal in my place or that some poor benighted soul had stuck a gun in Eddie's back and had been half kicked to death, but somehow I had an inkling that these facts were not unknown to him. Weber looked at me steadily and behind his eyeballs I thought I could sense a little smile, but it wasn't a friendly smile.

"It wasn't too difficult," I told him.

Weber leaned toward me and lowered his voice. "Will two thousand be all right again?"

"What about including expenses this time?"

"I was about to suggest the very thing," said Weber.

"And when will this be?"

"Tuesday at eight o'clock. I'll call you early in the afternoon and give you the name of the hotel. You didn't have any trouble getting around Montreal last time?"

"Nope."

"Not in the least?"

"It was a piece of cake, just like you said."

"It sounds like we're establishing a relationship." Weber smiled one of his humorless smiles. It was like a happy face drawn on an ice cube.

After leaving the Parting Glass, I drove out to Rosemary's. My Louisville slugger was sitting next to me in the Mercedes and I told myself I had some serious work to do, what I call the Triple Crown of automotive punishment: windows, headlights and taillights. But when I got out to the lunch counter, the Dodge was gone and Rosemary's Crown Victoria was parked in its usual place by the front door. Her little house was dark. I pulled up along the side of Route 29 and tried to decide what to do next. In the past, I had often bombed into Rosemary's when all her lights had been out and she was asleep and we had our pleasures nonetheless. But I knew if I woke her now, I wouldn't be able to keep the anger and disappointment out of my voice. Who's the bozo in the Dodge? I might say.

You ask, why not push her to the wall and read your list of charges? But this business of the strange car and my blossoming jealousy had made me redefine my feelings about the Queen of Softness. Redefine and clarify. If I bombed into her little house and made a scene, what was to say she wouldn't kick me out and refuse to see me again? I realized I had to be subtle. But here was a major problem. Vic Plotz has many gifts—more than your average Joe—but subtlety isn't among them. Consequently, I decided to drive back to Saratoga and add up the pros and cons and consider my various courses of action. Impulsive, that's me, and I had to work to find ways to outwit my own impetuous nature.

Monday morning I rolled out of bed at seven thirty, made myself a few strong cups of java and decided to trot out to Ballston Spa to visit Eddie Gillespie. Even though his previous trip to Montreal had contained a wrinkle or two, I couldn't believe that he would miss the chance of making himself another Cleveland. I knew how Eddie's mind operated. He would see himself as having made a thousand smackers for less than eight hours' work and already he would be estimating a yearly salary of four hundred grand.

Sad to say, I was mistaken.

When I got to Eddie's house, his wife Irene and baby Angelina were fretting in the kitchen and Eddie was still upstairs in bed. Not only was he in bed but he had pulled two or three pillows over his head and the only visible part of him was his big feet sticking out from under a gigantic Mickey Mouse comforter like two skinned puppies.

"Go away," he said, his voice muffled by the pillows.

"Eddie, I got a job for you."

"No more jobs," he said. "I'm not leaving the house."

"Eddie, it's good money."

"There's stuff more important than money."

It was hard to hear him speaking through three pillows. He sounded very far away.

"What's more important than money, Eddie?"

He said something that sounded like "Errr."

"Eddie, I can't hear you! What's more important than money?"

"Err! Errr!"

"What?" I shouted. I reached over and yanked the pillow off his head. What a shock! Eddie was as bald as a baby bird.

"Hair, hair!" he bellowed.

We stared at each other, then he shut his eyes and put his hands over his pasty white dome, which was flecked with a dozen red spots and lots of long pink scratches. Bereft of hair, his ears looked as big as sails.

"New fashion statement?" I asked.

He shook his head, keeping his fingers interlaced across his scalp.

"In disguise? Summer haircut? Imitating a cue ball?"

Eddie gave me a baleful look. "Lice," he mumbled.

Oh, how the proud are cast down! I wanted to raise my hands, drop to my knees and shout hallelujah but I was afraid that Eddie might find it in bad taste and I still needed him to drive to Montreal. He had a lumpy skull. It made me realize why he kept his hair so thick. Like between his hair and his brain existed a complicated pattern of rumble strips. Seeing them, they made perfect sense to me. Rumble strips on the brain, why hadn't I realized earlier that had been Eddie's problem? And the ears as big as scallop shells didn't help either. They looked like a rudimentary air-conditioning unit, but only if he could flap them.

"Pick the lice up from darling Angelina?" I asked.

He looked furious. "I got them in Montreal. I *knew* I shouldn't have kicked that guy. I betrayed the whole spirit of my training. I gave way to violence and the pleasures of excessive force."

"Zapped by the ghost of Bruce Lee," I suggested.

Eddie sat up on the edge of his double bed and looked at me as if I were one of the mentally challenged who was jumbling a problem in simple arithmetic: two plus two spells *cat.* "I feel sorry for you, Victor. What will you do when the Buddha presses his thumb against your forehead to make it clear that you have been following the wrong path?"

"I expect I will take a dump in my pants. I scare easy." It was hard to look at Eddie's white skull, it was too shiny. I found myself regretting the absence of his black locks.

"If I was as old as you," said Eddie in a superior manner, "I'd be more careful with my talk. Aren't you worried about what you'll say to your maker? You're a lot closer to him than I am."

Eddie gave me a prissy look. I was in a difficult position. I knew I could reduce him to a quivering mass of pain with only a few chosen words, but then who would drive to Montreal?

"Eddie, my heart goes out to you in your recent loss, but the news is not all bad. How would you like to make another thousand bucks?"

"Would it mean going up to Montreal?"

"See it as another little ride in the Mercedes."

"I'd rather put my head in the microwave. Can't you understand? I've betrayed everything important to me. Not only did I kick that guy, I liked doing it. You think the knowledge of my wrongs can be wiped away with another thousand bucks?"

"It's worth a try."

Eddie lay back down on the bed. Once again he flopped the pillow over his shining skull. It was like seeing the sun go behind a cloud. To tell the truth, I wasn't sorry to see it disappear. "Eddie," I said, "Does this mean no?"

"Err," said Eddie, "err, errr!"

I figured this was where I came in so I made my departure.

Downstairs Irene was dusting the philodendrons. She was a cute little number who liked to wear hot pants to do the housework, but like many modern women she was too scrawny: one more potential beauty who had wrecked her body through aerobics.

"Tell me," I said, "did Eddie really pick up lice in Montreal?"

Irene pursed her ruby lips as if about to spit out a fly that had inadvertently found its way into her mouth. "He got the bugs from Angelina. Half the kids in daycare have them. All their heads got shaved."

"Then what's this business with Montreal?"

"It's easier for him to blame what he dislikes than to blame what he loves."

I gave her a look: hot pants, tank top, dark ringlets born to be tossed, thick red lipstick. She was like Socrates in drag.

"You said a mouthful," I said.

"Somebody has to."

An hour later I was in Charlie's office. I had picked up coffee and cinnamon raisin bagels from Bruehegger's Bagel Bakery. I had bought the *New York Times*, which Charlie likes to take a peek at but feels he cannot afford on a regular basis, and I even obtained a little pot of purple crocuses to bring some cheer to his dreary surroundings. If you think all this was intended to be a complicated bribe, you are correct. But one of the things I like about Charlie is that he can always take you by surprise. It turned out the bribe was unnecessary and I wondered if I could sell the crocuses back to the florist.

"I'd be glad to go up to Montreal with you," he said, nibbling on a bagel. Charlie has an old plaid porkpie hat that he likes to wear and it sat on his desk bathed in sunlight.

"Would you really?"

"There's something funny going on with Weber and I'm curious. When do we go?"

"Do you think someone will try and stick us up?"

"Maybe. Certainly, we'll have to be prepared."

"Does that mean I get to carry a gun?"

"No, but I might bring one along."

Then we settled down to discuss what had to be done.

These were exciting prospects and for the next twenty-four hours I was all aflutter. Little scenarios buzzed through my brain about the villains trying this move or that move and I would disarm them with graceful gestures that I had seen in kung fu movies but had never tried myself. In truth, the side of my hand is as soft as last year's banana and why I thought I could use it to cut down trees, I don't know. I would look at myself in the mirror a dozen times a day to see if I looked any tougher. I even made growling noises at the cat.

During this time I dropped in on the Queen of Softness at odd hours to see if I could catch her doing something she shouldn't. I never did. Mostly she was pleased to see me, though once she looked at me with a concern that I first thought was guilt, then realized showed anxiety for my mental condition. I myself admit that I was acting strange, but I had never truly experienced jealousy and it made me feel like a kid again. There is nothing like jealousy to revive the vital body fluids. And I would also fantasize about catching some big bozo peeling the Queen of Softness like Samson used to peel grapes, ripping his head from his torso and slam-dunking it into a squirrel's nest in the old oak tree behind her house. As for the Dodge with the horizontal taillights, I didn't see it, but I had no doubt it would show up again.

This time the pickup was at the Holiday Inn Crowne Plaza on Sherbrooke, which made me feel good because just how strange could a Holiday Inn be? Because we wanted to make it seem that

I was driving up to Montreal by myself, Charlie met me in Glens Falls at the Queensbury Hotel, about twenty miles north of Saratoga. He had brought a revolver, an old snub-nosed .38 that he felt sentimental about because he used to carry it when he was a Saratoga cop. On this trip, he stashed it in the trunk so we wouldn't have any trouble getting through customs.

Driving north from Saratoga is peculiar. The landscape gets more mountainous and less populated and it feels you are driving to the ends of the earth, but then you pass through it, like passing through a door, and you come to a whole new country packed with people who haven't learned to speak English yet. Charlie and I talked about horse races of the past, races where our favorites were beaten by a whisker or sat down on the track for no apparent reason or paused to sniff the posies. We talked, in fact, to keep from thinking.

I got to say I felt jumpy. Eddie hadn't said much about the guy he had beaten up except that he was big, and I must have thought a hundred times: just how big is big? And each time I thought it, the guy got bigger. As for Eddie, Charlie had seen him and reported that he still refused to get out of bed.

"I promised to drive down to Albany tomorrow," said Charlie, "and buy him a nice wig."

"Eddie with a rug," I said, "it makes you philosophical."

"He warned us to watch out for ourselves in Montreal—hairwise, that is."

"If going bald was the worst thing that Montreal had to offer, I'd feel greatly comforted."

Once we got through customs, Charlie retrieved his revolver from the trunk. Both of us were slightly miffed that customs didn't take the slightest interest in us. As we kept driving north, we could see Montreal in the distance: big and ominous.

But who am I kidding. Absolutely nothing happened. We came off the expressway on rue University, drove ten blocks and there was the Holiday Inn. At eight o'clock I handed in the claim check to the concierge and picked up the suitcase: a battered black leather bag with a substantial weight to it. I went back to the parking garage with Charlie tailing fifteen feet behind me. He wore his porkpie hat so I had no trouble locating him when there were people around. It was cold and snowy but between us we probably sweated a couple of quarts of salt water. I jumped in the car and started up; a minute later Charlie jumped in beside me. Five minutes after that the Mercedes was heading back out rue University.

"A piece of cake," said Charlie.

"I'll feel better when we make it across the border."

But then we crossed the border and still nothing happened. As we drove the rest of the way down to Saratoga, I felt good but I also felt like a guy who had been stood up, like I wasn't good enough to rob.

"Trying to rob Eddie must have been an isolated incident," I suggested.

"Maybe." Charlie seemed thoughtful.

"I'll still give you a thousand bucks, even though you didn't have to defend me or nothing."

"That's nice of you," said Charlie.

"Unless of course you feel you don't deserve the thousand bucks, in which case I'd be glad to pay you five hundred."

"No," said Charlie, "I feel I deserve the thousand." He looked out the window for a moment. It was dark and the only traffic was big trucks. Snow skittered across the highway and reflected in the headlights. Then Charlie said, "But if this was such a piece of cake, then why couldn't Weber have used one of his regular couriers?"

"Maybe they were indisposed."

"I checked. They weren't."

"Maybe Weber likes me. Maybe he trusts me. You know, older man to older man."

I could see Charlie looking at me but he didn't say anything. I felt he didn't trust himself to say anything.

"If I do this once a week for a year," I said, "then I can get myself a new Mercedes."

Again Charlie looked as if he were tempted to say something not entirely polite, but he forbore.

When we got to Glens Falls, Charlie said, "I want to take a look at that suitcase."

I'd parked next to Charlie's Mazda 323, which was parked in the lot back behind the Queensbury Hotel. Charlie fished the suitcase out of the backseat. It was unlocked, which surprised me, but obviously it had to be unlocked if we were going to get it through customs. He opened it and there were some smelly old shirts and smelly underwear.

"Maybe you need gloves," I said, opening the window a crack.

Charlie dug under the clothes to the false bottom. Of course it didn't look false, it looked like the bottom of the suitcase, but if you compared the inside with the outside you could see there was a difference of three inches. Charlie took out his Swiss Army knife, fiddled with the edges and after a moment the false bottom popped open. Underneath was a pretty sight: stacks of one-hundred-dollar bills lying in rows as if snoozing: two rows by five rows and in each stack was twenty-five bills for a total of two hundred and fifty thousand.

"What do you say that you and me run away to Costa Rica," I suggested.

"Your tastes are too pricey," said Charlie. "This money would last you only a couple of weeks." He took out a stack from the middle, then slipped a hundred-dollar bill out of the bottom.

"Jeez, Charlie, you're not going to steal it, are you?"

"Nope." Charlie got out of the car and went into the hotel. Five minutes later he returned. Once he was settled again in the front seat, he put two one-hundred-dollar bills on the seat between us.

"Can you tell which one came out of the suitcase?" he asked.

"One of them's a little bent."

"Let's hope Mr. Weber doesn't notice," said Charlie. He slipped the bill into the bottom of the packet and returned it to its original position in the suitcase. Then he took the other hundred-dollar bill, folded it and put it in his shirt pocket.

"You better hurry if you want to get to Weber's by eleven o'clock," he said as he got out of the Mercedes.

"And what're you going to do with that hundred smackers?"

"A little experiment." Charlie gave me a smile that showed his teeth, doffed his porkpie in my direction and shut the door of the Mercedes.

I like to think that all of our troubles began with that little experiment, but of course they started before. But not long before, maybe only a week or two. I wouldn't want you to think, as some people have suggested, that they began the very day I was born.

■ FIVE ■

The next morning, Wednesday, around nine o'clock I drove out to the Queen of Softness's diner for breakfast, even though she refuses to serve me anything other than All-Bran, a bran muffin and Postum. No bacon and eggs for her sweetie. It was a sunny morning but cold. The snow in the fields was shiny with light so the very air was luminous. Fence posts wore little hats of snow. I kept my eyes out for robins, which for me were positive reinforcement that spring was coming. No robin, no spring—that's how I see it.

Ten cars and pickups were parked in front of the diner. I looked for the suspicious Dodge but, not finding it, I heaved a little sigh. I tromped through the slush to the front door, pushed my way in and was met by hillbilly music, the smell of sizzling bacon and burned coffee. That last surprised me because Rosemary was always particular about her coffee. Glancing around, however, I realized that Rosemary was not in residence. She's got a tall chair behind the cash register, like a black bar stool with a back and a chromium footrest. She likes to sit on it like a queen. At the moment it was vacant. Old Ernie Boner (his real name is Bonowski) was making eggs and Henrietta was slinging hash. Henrietta has slung hash for Rosemary for about six years. She is one of those skinny women who is always rushing around and who thinks herself too fat, consequently she eats about two cornflakes a day. Maybe she's thirty-five. She also chain-smokes and talks a lot about letting her hair down, which is hard to imagine because her hair is very short. It is also orange.

"Rosemary called from Albany," Henrietta told me. "She's stuck down there. She's been stuck all night."

I don't know about you, but sometimes a word or two will give me a visual image—it will pop right into my head—and the visual image I got was of two dogs being stuck together after screwing. You know how they can be stuck together for hours until you have to come along and give one of the dogs a kick in the pants? That's the image I got of the Queen of Softness being stuck in Albany.

"Aha," I said.

"Her car broke down," said Henrietta. I was sitting at the counter and Henrietta stood on the other side of it, already pouring me coffee. She knows I hate Postum.

"Her car broke down and she's stuck in Albany," I said.

"That about sums it up," said Henrietta.

"And she was stuck all night," I said.

"Look at the bright side," said Henrietta, "I'll give you the breakfast special and Rosemary will never know: four eggs sunny side up, a pound of home fries and seconds on bacon."

"You think she could smell it on my breath?"

"Just don't forget to brush," said Henrietta. "You want to start off with a big slice of Boston cream pie?"

I asked for orange juice instead and Henrietta hurried off. She likes to jog on the job. She wears a white uniform with her name in red lettering on the left breast pocket, except her name is too long for the pocket, so it only says, "Henriet," which leads a lot of truckers who are trying to pick her up to say, "That's a real pretty name, it must be French."

I sipped my coffee and brooded about Rosemary being stuck in Albany. Of course I had no doubt that she was getting schtumphed by the guy in the Dodge. It seemed I was receiving a lesson in life that I had momentarily forgotten but which, in fact, I had always known. Even tutti frutti turns to vanilla from overuse. The Queen of Softness needed sharper tastes in her life. Stronger music, louder wine and spangles on the bare surfaces. Couldn't I understand that? Sure I could. It was time for old Vic to pack up his condoms and tiptoe away. Although first, of course, I was going to catch the fellow in the Dodge, put his pecker in a toaster and make it fry. I would be happy to forgive and forget, but only after.

I ate my eggs, home fries and bacon but the joy had gone out of them. It wasn't even any fun sticking the yolks with the point of the knife to see them ooze.

Henrietta watched me pecking at my plate. "Off your feed?" she asked.

"I got a bug."

She nodded sympathetically. "I been there myself."

Around ten I drove back to Saratoga Springs. Although it was still sunny, the brilliance had gone out of the day. I was looking out through sad-colored glasses. I began to think about retirement communities in North Carolina and whether I should really give my body to the University of Chicago. Let's face facts, there was a shroud across the sun and woe was my only pal.

Maybe it was this that kept me from paying attention. Maybe I would have been more alert in a happier state. Wouldn't I have at least noticed that the door of my apartment was unlocked? I pushed open the door without much thought, then the world grabbed my attention at last. Like someone had picked up my apartment, shaken it fiercely and dumped it upside down. Or maybe one of those Texas tornadoes had slipped into the fifth dimension, exited into my apartment and banged around for a while. The place, let me tell you, was a mess.

It took me a minute to realize someone had been searching for something. All the drawers had been pulled out and their contents were scattered on the floor. And the kitchen cabinets had been emptied and the spoons, forks and knives were scattered across the linoleum. The closets had been emptied of my nice gray suits and the suits themselves had been searched, their pockets turned inside out and in some cases ripped out. The cushions were dumped from the sofa and armchair and most of the furniture was topsy-turvy. Even Moshe III's catbox had been tipped over in the bathroom. A box of Tide had been emptied. The ceiling lights had been pulled down. Pictures had been taken from the walls, photographs had been removed from their frames.

Moshe III came out of the closet and wound himself around my legs. Even the cat was in a state of shock. I stood in the middle of my living room trying not to step on stuff, because that was what I had now: not proud possessions but stuff. Not only had my apartment been searched, it had been searched maliciously. It was both search and punishment. This was a sobering thought. And into my dim brain sprang the idea that the only person who could be responsible for this was the guy in the Dodge who had been paying visits to Rosemary. Silly, of course.

I picked up the armchair, turned it over, replaced the cushion and sat down. Moshe III jumped up on my lap. I would have made myself a cup of coffee but all the coffee had been dumped on the floor. I would have poured myself a glass of milk but the milk was on the floor as well. I sat and thought about karma and how sometimes it can come along and give you a whack in the chops. I must have been thinking pretty hard because when I looked up I saw two guys standing in the doorway. They each had an arm around the other's shoulders. They were looking at me and grinning and nudging each other in the ribs with stumpy fingers.

These two guys had short black bristly hair and they wore black weight-lifter pants and black T-shirts and black leather jackets and on their feet were great big white basketball shoes with the laces hanging loose. They were probably in their late thirties. They looked like professional movers, I mean, house movers, furniture movers. They kept nudging each other and grinning.

"He's home," said one.

"Welcome back," said the other.

"And he's sitting down," said one.

"That makes it easier," said the other.

The first one gestured around to my apartment. He had a little goatee that wasn't so much a goatee as designer stubble. "Like what we done?" he asked.

The other was clean-shaven. He gave another smile. "Takes practice, a job like this. You can't just come in and hope to do it on your first try. You got to know what to wreck first. It's got a special order to it."

"It takes verve," said the guy with the stubble.

"Pizzazz," said the other.

"Who are you guys?" I asked. They looked as benign as two Santas, but Moshe III had scampered off my lap and disappeared. This was not a happy sign because it suggested prior knowledge on his part.

"He wants to know who we are," said the one with the stubble.

"He thinks he can ask questions," said the other. He pronounced it "axe."

"You know," said Stubble, "some guys were just born to have the shit kicked out of them."

"And stomped," said the other. "Like the world is divided into stompers and stompees and he's a stompee." He pronounced it "woild."

Now this was not happy talk even though my visitors were smiling. I wondered why I had never installed an alarm system in my apartment with a horn on top of the building that could bellow "Help! Help!"

"Okay, Pudge, get up and take off your clothes," said Stubble.

"I beg your pardon," I said, being polite.

"I like that," said Stubble, "he can beg."

"It shows class," said the other one.

Stubble looked at me and his face turned red. "Get the fuck on your feet you old fart and strip off your clothes!"

I guess I was in a state of shock because I didn't move fast enough. Stubble took a couple of steps forward, yanked me to my feet and head-bopped me so I fell down again. Then the other one gave me a kick in the butt that hurt.

"Soft," he said. Then he kicked me again.

"We will repeat our request," said Stubble. "Stand up and take off your clothes."

I was wearing a gray suit, a gray tie and a dove gray shirt. Like gray is my little affectation, and as I began to strip off my clothes, I began to think it was a trifle silly.

"You can leave on your underpants," said Stubble. "We don't want to see your dong."

"It's probably gray as well," said the other one.

They laughed.

In less than a minute I was standing there wearing nothing but my Jockey shorts, which were red.

"Cute shorts, Pudge," said Stubble.

"Pudge is a fancy dresser," said the other one, picking up my suit coat. "Feel this material. I like fancy dressers." He reached into the coat. There was a rip and his hand emerged holding the inside pocket. "Ooops," he said, "shoddy materials after all."

The two men proceeded to search my clothes. They emptied the contents of my pockets on the floor. They emptied my wallet. A couple of times I heard fabric rip. It wasn't particularly cold, but I was shivering. They searched my shoes, they searched my socks, they searched my dove gray fedora, leaving it mashed on the floor.

"How about a rectal search?" said Stubble. He gestured to the fireplace set. "We could use the poker."

"I say we give Pudge the benefit of the doubt," said the other one.

Stubble took the poker and slapped the hooked end into his palm. "We could just root around a little," he said.

"Hasn't Pudge been okay with us?" said the other. "Hasn't he been the perfect gentleman? I say we call it a day." He pronounced it "poifict."

"No pain?" asked Stubble.

"We don't always need pain," said the other.

"It's fun sometimes," said Stubble.

"True, but we got to put the job above the fun. After all, the job comes first."

Stubble scratched his chin. "I guess I'm only thinking of myself."

"I forgive you," said the other guy.

Stubble took a few steps toward me. I worked hard to keep from shutting my eyes. Instead, I stared down at his basketball shoes. Stubble reached out and patted my cheek twice. "I bet you hope you never see us again," he said. "But I bet you're wrong. Guys like you, Pudge, it always takes a while to catch on. Remember," he gave me a wink, "next time the rectal search."

Then they were gone. I guess they must have actually walked out the door, but maybe they just blinked out like a light blinks out. I made a jump for the phone and called Charlie at his office. I got his answering machine. So I called him at Janey's and got the answering machine there as well. So I called him at the lake and again got the machine. On all three machines I put the same message: "Charlie, I need help. Bring your gun."

Then I got dressed again, putting on clothes that weren't ripped. I was in a state of shock, but I don't want you to think I'm tugging at your tear ducts. My body felt deeply offended. I buttoned my shirt, got the buttons all wrong, then had to button it up again. I even had trouble tying my shoes. I had no doubt that if those guys had the least desire to do a rectal search with the poker, they would have done it. I like to think of myself as someone who plays it fast and loose, but Stubble and his pal made me look like Mother Teresa, or almost.

I sat down again and stared at the wreckage of my apartment.

Moshe III came crawling out from someplace and hopped up on my lap, but he didn't purr. He was too worried to purr. Even the plants had been emptied out on the rug, for Pete's sake. If I was upset, my begonia was worse.

I was sitting there thinking of my sins and wondering which had led to my current trouble when there was a knock on the door. Charlie, I said to myself, and I jumped to my feet.

But it wasn't Charlie, it was old man Weber.

"I'm afraid I don't have time to talk right now," I said.

Weber gave me a smile. His teeth had a pleasant yellow tint. "I'm afraid you don't have any choice."

"That's what you think." I began to shut the door.

"Would you like the boys to pay another visit?"

I stopped shutting the door. "Those bozos work for you?"

"Let's say they are of my acquaintance," said Weber.

I stood back to let him in. "Don't ask for a cup of coffee. They threw my coffee on the floor."

"I always find that impetuosity conceals a caring heart," said Weber, glancing around my apartment.

I picked up a straight chair and set it in front of him. "In this case you may be mistaken."

Weber sat down and I sat down as well. He was wearing a dark suit and there was dandruff on the shoulders. He poked at one of my shirts—half a shirt actually—with his cane. "They appear to have been thorough."

"I don't know what they were looking for."

Weber had light gray eyes that reminded me of the marbles I played with when I was a kid. "They were looking for a hundred-dollar bill."

I can't say that a bell went off in my brain but there was a rudimentary tintinnabulation. "Money," I said.

"Not just money, a specific hundred-dollar bill. The bill you took from the strongbox last night."

Now the bell began to ring. "But it was replaced."

"That's irrelevant," said Weber. "The point is that you opened the suitcase, opened the false bottom and removed a bill.

So what if you replaced it with another? It was an act of arrogance on your part. Now you strike me as an intelligent human being. What are the consequences of arrogance?"

I thought a moment. "Two bozos show up and whop you?"

"Crudely put, but true nonetheless. However, from what I gather, they did not find the bill. Where is it?"

"I don't have it."

"Did you spend it?"

"No, I didn't spend it."

"Did you put it in the bank?"

"I didn't put it in the bank."

Old man Weber positioned his cane at his side, levered himself to his feet and slowly began walking toward the door.

"Where're you going?" I asked.

There was a touch of sadness in his eyes, but only a touch. "I'm going to get the boys. They said they'd softened you up, but I believe you can be made softer yet."

"Wait!" I said. "I can explain." Then I stood there with my mouth open as I tried to figure out what to say.

There was a knock on the door.

"I'll tell, I'll tell!" I said.

But it wasn't the boys, it was my pal Charlie Bradshaw.

"Victor, are you all right? I got your message." He looked worried. Charlie wore a dark blue down jacket that made him look like the Pillsbury Doughboy, and on his head was his pork-pie hat.

I introduced him to Weber. I figured both men already knew each other, but they shook hands, though not with a lot of warmth. Charlie kept looking around my apartment.

"What happened here?" he asked. There was a hush to his voice suggestive of awe.

"A couple of Weber's friends busted it up, then they tried to bust me up as well."

"Not my friends, Mr. Plotz, merely acquaintances. Business acquaintances but they are not in my employ."

We stood by the door. Charlie kept staring around. Weber kept his eyes on Charlie.

"What in the world were they looking for?" asked Charlie. He raised an eyebrow at me and I guessed he already knew what they were looking for.

"A hundred-dollar bill," I said. "Mr. Weber says it belonged to him. He's very particular about getting back his very own specific hundred-dollar bill."

"Nothing could be easier," said Charlie. He reached under his down jacket and extracted the hundred-dollar bill, which was folded vertically across Benjamin Franklin's nose. He handed it to Weber.

"Much obliged," said Weber.

"Happy to be of service," said Charlie.

I was getting a little miffed. "Jesus, Charlie, what's going on? Why's he want the bill back in the first place?"

"He wants the bill," said Charlie, "because it's counterfeit."

"I think I should make a telephone call," said Weber, "just so the boys don't visit us again. We need to talk."

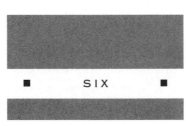

■ SIX ■

Fifteen minutes later old man Weber, Charlie and myself were seated at my round oak table, which was back on its feet— though a trifle wobbly—drinking tea and having a chat. Actually, I was surprised that Weber's fierce chums hadn't sliced open the tea bags. I am not much of a tea drinker but I fortified my cup with a little Jack Daniel's.

Weber was saying, "The trouble is, if you report me for the possession of counterfeit money, I will report you for smuggling it into the country. In fact, I will do more than report you."

I sat back and tugged at my gray locks. The conversation had taken a gloomy turn. Charlie stared into his cup as if trying to read his future in the tea bag.

"What about Eddie Gillespie?" asked Charlie, lifting his head. "Was he bringing in counterfeit money as well?"

By this question you will understand that we had already explained to Weber about Eddie Gillespie. It surprised neither of us to learn that he already knew about Eddie.

"That was the real stuff," said Weber. "The only time I have dealt with counterfeit money was last night. I should say that circumstances drove me to it."

"Perhaps you can explain," said Charlie.

"I'd rather not," said Weber. He picked something out of his ear and studied the result, giving it all the attention that Thomas Edison gave the lightbulb.

Moshe III wandered under the table and began rubbing against Charlie's legs. Charlie sneezed, then blew his nose.

"Even though we brought the money across the border," said Charlie, "we didn't know it was counterfeit. The police will believe that. I work with them often."

I stared at Charlie with admiration. Though he sometimes worked with the police, they absolutely hated him. They don't like the way he looks, they don't like the way he talks, they don't like the way he acts and they don't like the way he beats them at their own game. If the local cops thought they could put Charlie (and myself) away on a questionable charge, they would leap gazelle-like at the chance. The acting chief—a weight-lifting monster named Ron "No-Neck" Novack—despises Charlie. I heard it said that he likes to make paper dolls, write Charlie's name across their torsos, then ignite them with his Zippo.

Even Weber had an inkling of this because he said, "You're not so popular. Vic Plotz fucked up Peterson's parade."

"It was entirely accidental," I said. Through pure inadvertency I had ridden a horse the wrong way through the ex–police chief's retirement parade and a few people—malcontents one and all—had complained.

"Look, Mr. Weber," said Charlie, "I may not know what's going on but I can see that the two men who scared Victor don't work for you and that you're as frightened of them as he is. So I'd like to hear more about that counterfeit money and who it went to."

This was what I thought of as Charlie's Sincerity Mode. He had taken off his hat and leaned toward Weber across the table, glomming onto him with his baby blue eyes. It was, oddly enough, perfectly sincere, which was probably why it worked. Weber lifted his hands and pushed his palms toward us. "This could get us killed."

"And you think you'll be safe if you stay quiet?" said Charlie. "This involves your son, doesn't it?"

Weber's face went all crinkly and his eyes moistened. "My son's a fuckup."

"Joey," I said.

Weber nodded. After a moment he dragged a gray handkerchief out of his pocket and honked a foghorn noise into it that made his white hair quiver as if in a spring breeze. Charlie and I waited. Out on Broadway a siren went past.

Weber shoved his handkerchief back in his pocket. "Even though he's a fuckup, he's not a bad boy. Some kids get pimples, Joey didn't get the pimples but he's a fuckup. Maybe his mother spoiled him. Maybe I was too tough on him. When he graduated from high school, I felt he'd climbed a Himalaya on his hands and knees. He's not dumb, but he's easily distracted."

Charlie and I continued to wait. I knew Joey a little. He was a big sloppy kid who hung around the bars and bet on bad horses. In fact, if you had a question about a horse, you only had to ask Joey if he was betting on it to steer clear, since his horses always lost. And Joey was always asking to be introduced to broads and if he could buy you a drink, and he told a lot of jokes but his jokes were lousy and he always messed up the punch line ("Now what was it that hit the fan?"). I guessed he was about twenty-two. You hear about guys having two left feet, Joey had seventeen left feet. He was the kind of person you felt sorry for until he opened his mouth, then you wished he would go away. Despite this, he was the watermelon of his papa's eye.

"The trouble started," Weber said, "when Joey fell in love. And if anybody should be punished in this whole business, it's the woman who messed him up."

Why was it that for a split second I thought he was talking about the Queen of Softness? It must be an axiom: when you got woman troubles, it seems all you ever hear about are woman troubles.

"Who was she?" asked Charlie.

Weber stared at the backs of his hands. They were wrinkled and had liver spots but otherwise they looked like regular hands. "Some broad he met someplace. Her name's Sheila."

"Where'd he meet her?" Charlie asked.

"A bar. Maybe the Turf, maybe Lilian's. I remember he told me he'd met this amazing woman: smart, good-looking, a spiffy dresser. He told me she liked him. I felt glad for him. Joey's always had trouble with women and now he'd found a broad who liked him. I'm sorry she didn't drop dead as a child."

"What's wrong with her?" I asked. I'd known some Sheilas in my time.

"She got her hooks in him, that's all. She got him to take her expensive places. She got him to give her gifts. I'd ask him if he couldn't find a cheaper girlfriend. Joey would say, 'She's the only one who's ever loved me.' Hell, she loved his wallet. She loved his credit cards. Joey himself, he was the guy who carried them. He was his money's form of transportation. But she flicked his switch. She made him feel like a million bucks and if he'd had a million bucks, he'd have spent every dime on her."

"Where's she live?" asked Charlie.

"North of Albany somewhere. One of those fancy apartment complexes right by the interstate so that people can get in and out in a hurry. Joey wanted to move down there as well, but I wouldn't let him."

"Didn't he have his own money?" I asked.

"He didn't have any money except for what I gave him, or at least that's what I thought."

"Are we getting to the circumstances that led you to deal in counterfeit money?" asked Charlie.

Weber wrinkled up his nose. "You could say that." He pushed

his hand through his white brush-cut and more dandruff plopped onto the shoulders of his dark suit.

"So Joey robbed you?" asked Charlie, quietly.

"No, he didn't really rob me."

"Who did Joey rob?" I asked.

Weber sucked his teeth and studied his fingernails. It seemed as if we had reached a conversational hurdle. He looked around at my broken furniture and the stuff scattered across the floor. For a moment he seemed almost apologetic, then his face got a trifle stony. "I run a complicated business," he said.

We waited.

"It entails a lot of buying and selling."

We continued to wait.

"Like I buy gold in one place and sell it in another place."

"By 'places,' " asked Charlie, "do you mean countries?"

"Right, countries. I buy gold in one country and sell it in another. All over the world. I buy coins. I buy silver. I buy a lot of it."

"And you have couriers to do the traveling?" said Charlie.

"You bet." Weber was warming to his subject. "As for me, I hate traveling. I even hate driving down to Albany. Even going across town can be too much for me."

"So what does this have to do with the complications of your business?" Charlie asked.

"Well, sometimes these deals come up fast and consequently sometimes I need a lot of money fast." Weber stopped and appeared to mull this over.

"Are you saying you had to take a partner?" asked Charlie.

"Right, a partner." Weber looked relieved.

"And sometimes this partner fronts you a whole lot of money?" asked Charlie.

"Right, a bundle."

"And sometimes a lot of money is made on this money?" asked Charlie.

"Right, a whole packet."

"And sometimes taxes aren't paid on this money?" suggested Charlie.

Weber's face, which had been looking increasingly hopeful, now looked downcast. "I wish you wouldn't put it that way."

"Then how would you put it?" asked Charlie.

"If we buy in Hong Kong and sell in Macao and buy again in Turkey, it's possible none of the money would ever get to the States. So why should the IRS care?"

"Is that what you think?" asked Charlie.

Weber looked at the ceiling and refused to commit himself.

"And maybe," said Charlie, "we're not only dealing with tax evasion, maybe we're also dealing with money laundering."

"The trouble with you," said Weber, suddenly angry, "is that you don't talk about this stuff with any subtlety."

"The mob," I said, catching on at last, "that's who employs those two bozos who scared me half to death. You're laundering money for the mob."

"Who?" asked Weber, innocent-like.

"So-lo-mi-o," I said.

"What?" asked Charlie.

"Ma-fi-o-so," I explained.

Weber began talking in a rush. "I deal with very few of them. Maybe with only one man in particular. And he's a decent gentlemen. I've known him a dozen years. He's been to my house. He's eaten at my table. He's a family man. . . ."

"And he employs those bozos who scared me half to death."

"They're eager," said Weber.

"They're sadistic," I said.

"Let's see if I've got this straight," said Charlie. "You buy and sell gold, silver and coins all over the world. At times you need a lot of money fast, so you have a silent partner who fronts you the money. In return, you launder money for him. . . ."

"Scrub his bucks," I said.

"You launder his money," continued Charlie. "So where does your son Joey come into all this?"

"Joey robbed him," said Weber.

"Ah," said Charlie.

"A tactical mistake," I suggested.

"He needed the money to spend on Sheila?" asked Charlie.

"She required a few items," said Weber, looking at his hands again.

"Jewels and furs," I offered. "Maybe a Corvette."

"Joey didn't take a lot of money all at once," said Weber. "But it added up to a bundle."

"The Sheilas of this world have big appetites," I said.

"And your partner was getting suspicious," said Charlie.

"He's not quite my partner," said Weber.

"Nonetheless—" began Charlie.

"Nonetheless," continued Weber, "the money had to be replaced."

"Let me tell you how you decided to do it," said Charlie. He pushed back his chair and sat up straight like a grade school kid preparing to spell "Mississippi." Charlie enjoys these little detective gambits. What is a private investigator but a guy who likes to think he has the edge on truth? And sometimes Charlie shows off. I don't blame him. Sometimes I like to show off as well.

"You had some money you had to bring down from Montreal," said Charlie, "so you decided to rob yourself. Obviously you couldn't use your regular couriers: one, they might recognize the robber; two, they're fairly tough. So you went out and hired someone you thought would be an obvious pushover. . . ."

"I'm beginning to resent this," I said, as a light started flickering in my brain.

"If you had known Victor," said Charlie, "you wouldn't have hired him. Not because he's tough, but because he's devious—"

"Jesus, Charlie—"

"And Victor, instead of going up to Montreal himself," said Charlie, "farmed the job out to someone else, who turned out to be very tough indeed. Was it Joey's wrist that got busted?"

Weber nodded glumly.

"No wonder you were disappointed when Victor showed up with the money," said Charlie.

"I was heartbroken," said Weber.

"What I'm not sure about," said Charlie, "is how we get to the counterfeit money."

Weber stuck his finger into his cup and stirred his tea, which had to be cold by now. "This guy I know—let's call him Louie—had begun to suspect my son was skimming the money. He was asking questions. So I figured I could rob myself, replace the money that Joey had taken and no one would be the wiser. . . ."

"Wouldn't you also be robbing Louie?" I asked.

"How would he know? And if my Louie believed that Plotz had been robbed, then he would assume it was Montreal hoods who'd done it. Montreal is full of hoods."

"You were taking a chance," said Charlie.

Weber elevated his scrawny shoulders. "I didn't see I had any choice."

"What happened when your plan failed?" asked Charlie.

"I had to throw myself on Louie's mercy. I told him everything. I said I'd do whatever he wanted." Weber was staring down at his hands again.

"Which meant?"

"Louie has been after me for some time to bring down some other money."

"Counterfeit money," said Charlie.

"I didn't ask. All I knew was that it came from Hong Kong."

"As opposed to Fort Knox," I suggested.

"Sure, as opposed to Fort Knox. That's all I knew," said Weber. "And I didn't want to know any more. And I didn't want to bring it down for him, because it's one thing to evade a little tax business, but it's another—"

"To peddle Hong Kong greenbacks," I said, helping him out.

"Right," said Weber. "Louie had been asking me and I'd been refusing. But now I was stuck. I had to admit to Louie that my own son had been robbing him and I had to beg him, go down on my fucking hands and knees and beg him not to hurt Joey. Hurt him, shit, Louie could have killed him no trouble."

"Even though he deserved it," I said.

"That's not true," said Weber. "The broad deserved it."

"And Louie said he wouldn't hurt your son as long as you brought this counterfeit money from Montreal," suggested Charlie.

"That's about it."

"Is your son still seeing Sheila?" I asked.

"She dumped him for a jockey, a short guy. Petey Loomis, you ever heard of him?"

Neither Charlie nor I had heard of Petey Loomis.

"He's not a winning jockey," said Weber. "He's one of the other ones."

"Where's the counterfeit money now?" asked Charlie.

"Louie's got it. He checked it out bill by bill. When he found out you'd swapped a bill on him, I thought he'd have a shit fit. Of course, he didn't know it was you, he thought it was Plotz. The thing is, I'm in over my head. Louie says I still owe him money and he says I got to do more trips, meaning he wants Plotz to do more trips for him."

"Fat chance," I said. "Smuggling counterfeit money is no wrist-slapper. They'd pack me away for a long time. How could I visit my grandkids?"

Weber reached down to his briefcase and took out a black rectangular object. It was a videotape. "This is a copy. It shows Plotz in Montreal. It shows him giving the claim check to the concierge and getting the suitcase. It shows him crossing the border. It shows him delivering the suitcase to my house."

There was a moment of silence during which I could hear the pigeons cooing on the window ledge.

"I've always wanted to be in films," I said, trying to look at the bright side.

"You want to see it?" asked Weber.

"Let's," said Charlie.

Fortunately, the big guys who had busted up my apartment hadn't smashed my TV. Charlie and I set my couch right side up and Weber took a seat. I stuck the tape in the VCR. I even offered to make popcorn but Weber and Charlie had become so

serious that they didn't even bother to tell me to shut up. The
screen began to flicker. We waited.

Why is it that even when seeing a snapshot of one's elegant
puss one feels the airy wing of fame brush lightly across one's dome?
Maybe it's the fact that I belong to a pre-video age that led me to receive such a thrill from watching Vic Plotz on TV, even though
these same scenes, witnessed by others, could get me twenty years
in the federal slammer. Was my hair brushed, was I looking my best?
There I strolled into the lobby of Montreal's Holiday Inn: a distin-
guished-looking gentlemen in a gray overcoat and a gray suit. A
number of people, both men and women, gave me appreciative
looks. And here I had thought I had been unnoticed! Perhaps when
one has that shadowy aesthetic appeal found only in the unusual
and brainy one can never be entirely unnoticed. And here I was receiving the black suitcase from the concierge. How he smiles at me.
Certainly he recognizes class when he sees it. The camera follows
me out of the lobby. More turned heads and appreciative looks. In
the background I see Charlie Bradshaw lurking behind a potted
palm but the camera passes right over him as someone unworthy of
notice. I even feel a moment of sympathy for my pal. I mean, he's
got the heart and soul of a star but he lacks the looks, the sizzle.

There are more shots of me walking to the Mercedes, picking
up Charlie and driving away. Even the Mercedes looks good: an
elegant older model. Then we had a further shot of us going
through customs and a last shot of me delivering the suitcase to
Weber's house, but it is dark and I can't be seen too well, though
I recognize the walk, the confident step. What gets left out is our
little stopover in Glens Falls, which, I thought, was just as well.

"Jesus," I said, when it's over, "can you get me some copies for
my family and friends?" I turned to Charlie. "You think I should
get a theatrical agent?"

"A lawyer would be more like it," he said, trying his little
joke. I knew he was miffed that he hadn't gotten top billing.

"So," said Weber, "Louie wants me to make another trip to
Montreal next week. As far as I can see, he's got no reason to let
me loose. I'll be doing this until I get caught."

"Who took the video?" said Charlie.

"Louie had it done."

"Good camera work," I said. "A really professional job."

"But what can we do?" said Charlie.

"You're the detective," said Weber. "You got to find a way to make him set me and Joey loose, set all four of us loose. But let me warn you, Louie is no dope. As for the guys that work for him . . ." Weber nodded toward the wreckage of my apartment. It was a gesture more eloquent than alphabets.

"Maybe I should visit Pittsburgh," I said.

Weber gave me an unfriendly smile. "You wouldn't even make it to the airport." He got to his feet. "I'll leave you with the video. Louie's got the original. When you have something to tell me, give me a call. Be careful what you say. I think my phone is tapped."

Charlie and I watched him head for the door: a little old guy with a cane who looked like a toothbrush. I had an ache in my duodenum, which I recognized as severe depression.

"I'll help you clean up," said Charlie. "Come on."

Until early afternoon we swept and filled trash bags and put furniture back in its place. During the cleaning we didn't talk much, or rather maybe a dozen times Charlie would say, "I know what we can do . . . no, that wouldn't work," or I would say, "Hey, why don't we . . . no, we'd only get shot." So we stuck to a companionable silence, punctuated by sighs and the odd shaking of the head. At last the call of the belly became too great for us and we headed out to Rosemary's diner.

■ SEVEN ■

We took the Mercedes out to Rosemary's since I don't fit comfortably into Charlie's Mazda. It was a sunny afternoon in the mid-forties and the snow was melting. The weeping willows were getting that slightly yellow cast they get in early spring, which indicates that their leaves are ready to pop forth and do operatic numbers. There seemed to be more birds and the birds seemed cheerful, unlike us.

"The difficulty with trying to make this Louie person leave Weber alone," said Charlie, "is that he has no reason to listen to us. We lack clout. If we get in his way, he can toss us to the cops or set his goons on us."

"At least jail would take care of my retirement worries," I said. "If I get sent to a federal prison, I only hope it's in Florida. You get health insurance in jail, right?"

"After a fashion," said Charlie.

When we entered the diner, Rosemary was back on her tall

stool behind the cash register. She was wearing a tiger-stripe blouse of some rayonlike material with the top two buttons undone. From twenty feet truckers could lob burgers down her cleavage. This had never bothered me before—it had even been a source of pride—but now, because of the doofus in the Dodge, I would have preferred if she had buttoned up. Jealousy was a new experience for me, like polio or nose cancer.

When Rosemary saw us, she jumped down from her chair to give the two of us a peck on the cheek. Her bosoms banged against our lapels. If she had any guilt about being stuck down in Albany, she didn't show it.

"I've only been back an hour," she said. "Henrietta said you'd been here for breakfast."

"Trouble in Albany?" I asked, as Charlie and I took our seats in a booth.

"An old girlfriend of mine fell off the wagon," she said, "and I spent the night trying to boost her back up. I hardly slept a wink." Rosemary gave a yawn and patted her ruby lips.

The wisecrack is for me a verbal embellishment that is both a source of pride and a terrible pitfall. Like I play the wisecrack like Glenn Gould played the piano. Yet everything I could think of saying was fraught with danger. Hardly slept a wink? Boost what back up? Consequently, I did no more than give an affable smile and appear to study the menu: a sheet of paper that I knew so well that I could have recited it while doing the bugaloo to "Tea for Two."

"She's a wonderful woman," said Charlie, as the Queen of Softness walked back to the cash register.

"Charlie," I said, "what would you do if you found out that Janey was getting her orifices plugged by a freelancer?"

Charlie gave me what I thought of as a shrewd look. "I guess I would be depressed."

"Is that all? Wouldn't you do anything?"

"I'd probably move out."

"Nothing more?"

"I'd try not to shoot the guy."

"Wouldn't you do anything to Janey?" I whispered.

"I don't think so. I love her. If she started having sex with someone else, I'd probably blame myself. Tell myself I wasn't good enough in bed or simply wasn't interesting enough as a person. As I say, I'd be depressed. Is everything all right between you and Rosemary?"

"Unexplained absences and mysterious visitors. There's a guy in a Dodge who's been cluttering up the neighborhood."

"Ahh," said Charlie. "You should ask her about it."

"I'm afraid what I'll find out."

We both had the low-cal salad plate and moped over our sprouts and chicken bits.

"Well," said Charlie, "look at the bright side. If we go to jail, then your romantic problems will be solved."

"So you don't plan to help old man Weber? You just mean to play possum till the big flat foot of the law comes along to give you a powerful kick?"

"No," said Charlie, "I think we should go have a chat with his son, Joey."

"Baa, baa, black sheep," I said.

"The very same," said Charlie.

I pushed my sprouts to the side of my plate. "Has it occurred to you," I said, "that sprouts are the only thing from the 1960s revolution to stay with us?"

"And tofu," said Charlie, making a face.

Recently on the TV I heard a fitness broad talking about people with apple shapes and pear shapes. Joey Weber had a pineapple shape and he was just as prickly. He still, as they say, had not dressed for the day.

It was the middle of the afternoon of that same Wednesday and Joey was waving his right hand at us. The hand and wrist had a lot of tape around it. Joey was shouting, "Did I deserve this? Did I deserve this?"

Charlie was being his most reasonable. "Surely when you point a gun at another human being you have to anticipate that unpleasant things may happen."

When Charlie talks like this I start thinking that he should sell funerals or used cars.

"My pop said it would be a piece of cake. I really feel abused."

"What's a piece of cake for one person," I said, adopting a mandarin mode of my own, "may be a dog turd for someone else."

"And look at this!" Joey pulled open his bathrobe. There on the sacred flesh were two large black-and-blue marks, one shaped like Louisiana and the other like Minnesota. Otherwise, the flesh was a pasty grayish pink. I thought it looked rather improved by these state-shaped marks of violence. They added color and contrast to what otherwise resembled cheap blotting paper.

It had taken three phone calls to find out where Joey lived: an upscale bachelor apartment on the east side of town off Lake Avenue. It was the kind of place that by all rights should have been a motel room because of the decor. Let's say it was a motel room with aspirations. The curtains were shut and the room was dim. The furniture looked rented and the only personal stamp that Joey had put on his domicile was a sink full of dirty dishes and a king-sized box of Froot Loops on the kitchen counter. The cereal box was the only reading material in evidence.

Joey Weber was scared. He hadn't wanted to let us into his apartment and he didn't want to talk. He didn't have the brains or the courage to be a crook. All he had was laziness. Like he was too lazy to find a regular job and so he looked for an easier way. Now he had gotten himself in a pickle. I felt certain that the two mean bozos who had visited me had also put a tablespoon of terror into Joey as well. After all, he had stolen money from the mob, and his dad's plan to make everything better had gone haywire. Joey saw himself as looking at death on one side and a jail cell on the other. He would have preferred to be in darkest Africa but here he was in Saratoga Springs being grilled by Charlie Bradshaw who, though not a cop, was coplike.

Joey wore a dark purple velour robe and sheepskin slippers. Since his wrist hurt I guess he felt he didn't need to get dressed. He had a soft round face that drooped. If the rest of us are descended from monkeys, Joey's primary ancestor was a marshmallow. He had chestnut hair with a bit of red, which he wore longish and which neatly followed the moonlike contours of his skull: evidence of a hairstylist rather than a barber. He was about six feet and easily weighed an eighth of a ton.

"I don't see why my dad ever got mixed up with these crooks," said Joey.

"How'd you manage to rob them?" asked Charlie, conversationally. He held his hat in his hands, slowly revolving it like a melancholy flywheel.

When Joey looked embarrassed his cheeks puffed out another two inches. "I knew where my dad kept the money in the house, so I slipped out a few bills now and then. I guess it added up."

"Especially if they were hundred-dollar bills," I said. "What did it amount to, ten grand?"

Joey puffed out his cheeks again. We stood by his front door. Nobody had made any move to sit down. Joey's hands were buried in the pockets of his robe. His shoulders were hunched, which made his neck disappear. He looked confused the way Chinese look Chinese, like it was his racial characteristic.

"What'd you do with the money?" asked Charlie.

"I'd prefer not to say."

"Girls," I grinned, "aren't they the very devil? Think of the trouble they cause us."

Joey got angry again. It was like watching an overripe banana trying to develop backbone. "You're talking about someone I love. She's not just a girl." Joey began to weep. He made a series of honking noises and if I hadn't seen the tears, I might have tried a Heimlich maneuver. The tears didn't run down Joey's cheeks, they popped horizontally out of his eyes. It was like seeing a broken pipe. Then Joey clamped down on the shutoff valve and the waterworks stopped. He sighed. I felt a trifle guilty. Charlie stared down at the floor.

"Who is this young lady?" asked Charlie, when he was sure the tears were over.

"I said, I don't want to talk about it."

"Come on, Joey," I said, "we don't have all day. We already

know about Sheila. My friend's being coy. You swiped the mob's money and spent it on a girl. What'd you buy her? Krugerrands?"

"Jewels, I expect," said Charlie. "Did Sheila like diamonds?"

"Emeralds," said Joey, in almost a whisper.

"How'd you have the nerve to take the money?" I asked.

"She said she was going to leave me," said Joey. "She said she loved me but she needed presents—"

"Like a car needs gas," I said.

"But she's not materialistic," said Joey, sotto voce. "She just didn't believe I really loved her."

"So she wanted proof?" I asked.

"Assurances," said Joey.

"Didn't you think you'd get in serious trouble and get your dad in trouble too?" asked Charlie in a kindly and inquisitive manner.

Joey shuffled his slippers. I was afraid he'd turn on the water-works again but he just snuffled. "I loved her. I still love her. We met at this bar, the Parting Glass. She liked me, she laughed at my jokes."

"That's a bad sign," I said.

Charlie hushed me. "And you began seeing each other?"

Charlie imagines sex to be an eye thing rather than a genital thing.

"Right away," said Joey, still in a subdued voice.

"And where is she now?" asked Charlie.

"I'm not sure."

Charlie's eyebrows went up. "What do you mean?"

"Her phone's been disconnected."

There was a pause as we considered the ramifications of this. Sheila had hit the trail.

"I don't suppose she returned the emeralds?" I asked.

Nobody bothered to answer.

"But she'll call eventually," said Joey, "I'm sure of it." He went back to shuffling his slippers on the carpet. Charlie patted his shoulder. That's the difference between us. I would have tossed a glass of water in Joey's face and told him to straighten up. Charlie was more of a worrier and encourager.

A few minutes later Charlie and I were heading back across town in the Mercedes. Like it was so steady that I could drive with just one finger on the top of the wheel. Nearly two hundred thousand miles and it still ran like a dream. But now it was my turn to be in a philosophical mood. "No doubt about it," I said, "romance fucks things up. It's like a mathematical puzzle, how do you take a complete loser like Joey Weber and make him even more of a loser? Romance, that's how."

"He probably meant well," suggested Charlie.

I gave him a critical look. "Joey was trying to think with his prick. Pricks aren't made to think with. It's like trying to play the 'Star-Spangled Banner' on a carrot. Hey!"

I made this startled remark because I had glanced into the mirror and all I could see was the big black grill of another car about five inches behind the Mercedes. Then there was a simultaneous crash and jolt, followed by the tinkling of falling glass and metal as my taillights sprinkled down onto the asphalt. Charlie and I were bounced back in our seats, then thrown forward against our seat belts.

"Jesus!" said Charlie, trying to turn around.

"My car!" I replied.

I looked again in the mirror and the vehicle behind me pulled back far enough so I could see it was a Chevy Blazer with a special oversized front bumper, what might be called a car-bashing bumper. Then I saw who was sitting in the front seat.

"Charlie, you want to take a gander at the guys who busted up my apartment?"

Charlie turned to stare through the back window. In my mirror, I could see the guy with the designer stubble and his rough buddy smiling and waving to us like old friends. They were also laughing and slapping each other on the shoulders. It was amazing how likable they appeared. Then the Blazer jumped forward again and I received another bash on my rear fender. Charlie and I were pushed back, then thrown forward again.

"But we're right downtown," said Charlie indignantly.

And that was the peculiar part, or part of the peculiar part. We were right on Union Avenue, with houses on both sides of the street and a few small stores. It was the middle of the afternoon. There were other cars around. On the sidewalks old folks were walking their dogs and moms were pushing strollers. A few crocuses were in evidence.

The thugs in the Blazer had pulled back and were grinning and waving again. The Blazer's big metal bumper seemed constructed from black steel rods. Stubble was driving. He tapped out a little rhythm on his horn: Shave and a haircut—two bits. Then they laughed again. Then they waved. Then the Blazer charged forward a third time and bashed me. The Mercedes veered and I brought it back straight. I figured the rear end of the Mercedes must look like a baby's creamy pink bottom after being nibbled by a pit bull.

"They're crazy," said Charlie. "They can't do this here!"

"You want to tell them," I said, "or shall I?"

"There's a cop," said Charlie. "Flash your lights."

Looking up, I saw a Saratoga Springs patrol car leisurely toodling toward us. I flicked my lights at him. At that moment the cheerful guy in the Blazer saw the cop car as well and made a hasty right turn. The policeman smiled and waved at us, figuring I must be a pal. After all, this was Saratoga, a nice place to live, a nice place to raise your kids.

"Should I get him to pull over?" I asked.

"Just wave and keep going," said Charlie, waving at the copper. I could see it was a red-haired doofus I'd known for many years by the name of Emmett Van Brunt.

"What about the Mercedes?" I asked.

"Isn't it insured?" Charlie's face was pale, a mixture of fading apprehension and increasing anger.

That kind of remark could only be made by someone who drives a little car like a Mazda or Toyota or Nissan, the kind of guy who doesn't realize that some cars have soul.

ddie Gillespie in a turban was something I had not figured to
see in this lifetime. Nor any other for that matter. It was a large
white affair, wrapped around and around—like a Sikh's, though
sicker. Eddie was quite proud of it, seeing it as a viable alternative
to hair.

"It's medicated," he told Charlie and me, then beamed. He
had moved from his bed to the living room reclino-rocker and
the darling Angelina was playing at his feet. She, too, wore a turban. It gave them a family resemblance, not that she needed one
since she also had his schnoz.

"Eddie," I said, "does this mean you no longer eat meat?"

"Oh," he said, "I eat plenty of meat. This is more of a health
statement than a religious statement. Just till the bugs are gone."

"Lice," said Charlie.

"The little fuckers," said Eddie. He looked guiltily at Angelina to see if she had overheard, but she was picking her nose
and couldn't be bothered.

In the kitchen, Eddie's wife Irene was whipping together a meat
loaf for dinner. She too was wearing a turban. Like I had entered the
Third World. It also made my scalp itch. Glancing at Charlie, on
the other end of the couch, I saw him furtively scratching his scalp
as well. I had a momentary vision of half of Saratoga wearing medicated turbans: cops and carpenters, priests and pimps.

It was late Wednesday afternoon and we'd been at Eddie's
little house in Ballston Spa for about five minutes, long enough
to turn down beers and coffee. Out at the curb the Mercedes was
parked with a sadly rumpled rump, maybe two grand worth of
work needed to be done. Although I was unhappy with Stubble
and his pal, I was also glad they had gone away. Guys with neither
restrictions nor scruples make me edgy. The sad part was that I
knew they hadn't gone away for good.

"We were wondering," said Charlie, "if you know a jockey
named Petey Loomis."

Eddie thoughtfully nodded his head and the turban nodded
with it. I realized what I disliked about the turban was that it gave

Eddie a completely bogus semblance of intelligence. I mean, Eddie was one of those guys that you can look into his left ear and see light pouring in from the right, or vice versa. Now he had an aura of wisdom.

"Petey Loomis," said Eddie, "the jockey."

"That's right," said Charlie.

"He's not a very good jockey," said Eddie.

"That's okay," said Charlie. "We just want to talk to him."

"He falls off the horses a lot," said Eddie.

"But he can still speak, can't he?" I asked. Talking to Eddie was like talking to an intelligent plant.

"Oh, he can talk all right," said Eddie. "I've heard him talk plenty. A real chatterbox."

"Where can he be found?" asked Charlie. I noticed he was scratching his scalp again. Both of us were dying to be out of there. I kept thinking I saw tiny little creatures moving on the arm of the sofa. Even my feet itched.

"I'm not exactly sure where he lives," said Eddie, staring at the ceiling. "It's not Saratoga Springs. It could be Clifton Park or someplace like that, unless he's moved."

I admired Charlie's patience. I felt ready to strike Eddie, but then I might get bugs on my hand.

"Doe he hang out anywhere in particular?" asked Charlie.

"Oh yeah," said Eddie, "he hangs out plenty."

"Where?" I asked, in spite of myself.

"I seen him in bars."

"Which bars?" I asked.

"Bars?" asked Eddie.

"Specific drinking places," I said.

"Well, I seen him in the Turf in Saratoga. He likes the Turf a lot."

In two minutes, Charlie and I were on our way.

■ EIGHT ■

There are two hundred bars in Saratoga Springs and so it was perhaps one more instance of bad karma that we should find Petey Loomis in the last bar in which we looked and the bar closest to Charlie's office, the Golden Grill, half a block away on the corner of Putnam and Phila. It was just another example of how the world is fucked up. We had looked east; we had looked west; and here was Petey Loomis smack in the center. As for Petey, he was half in the bag. He was a small jockey and it was a big bag.

The Golden Grill was a dark place and on busy nights people liked to dance. It was there I did my disco moves when my knees were not so iffy and my pelvis still rotated. Now they played rap. It was the nearest downtown Saratoga got to having a "black bar," though on this particular occasion only white folks were in evidence. It was around seven thirty and the streets were empty. Five drinkers were pushing the limits of their cocktail hour at the Golden Grill but Petey Loomis was drinking by him-self, sitting up on a couple of phone books. We sat down on ei-ther side of him.

"Buy you a cup of coffee?" Charlie asked.

Petey turned his head slowly toward Charlie, then he turned his head slowly toward me, then he turned his head toward Char-lie again. The expression on his round face was like the expres-sion on a cheap frying pan after you've burned your pan-fried steak: crusty. "Irish?" he asked.

He was maybe an inch under five feet and skinny. Nearly all jocks have to watch their weight, but you could see that wouldn't be Petey's problem. His problem was the booze. In fact, I later heard he had a little joke that he liked: when he was racing, he would hang around the scales slowly licking a double-dip ice cream cone. Most of the other jocks hadn't eaten all day and see-ing Petey with his fudge nut supreme with sugar doodads on top made their bellies kick up a ruckus. Petey would smirk. There was no lightness to Petey, no chipperness of soul—all his jokes were meant to turn the blade. He had long straight black hair and at the moment one wing of it covered his right eye. His left eye had a yellowish cast.

"I was thinking of black," said Charlie.

Petey returned to his drink, which appeared to be the rem-nants of a margarita. "Take a hike."

I figured there was racing at Aqueduct but maybe Petey didn't like New York or maybe he was taking a sabbatical. In looking for him at about fifty bars that afternoon, it had become clear he had few friends. In fact, most people couldn't stand him. "The little prick," was how he was most often described. Several bartenders had said how Petey was no longer welcome in their joints.

"How come?" Charlie had asked.

"Likes to break glass," had been the answer.

And this was the guy who Charlie wanted to tell all. Even with the telephone books, Petey didn't reach very high on the bar stool, but if he straightened his back then his lower lip could just reach the salty rim of his margarita glass. He seemed to like to rest it there.

"I was hoping you could tell us where we could find Sheila," said Charlie, still being Mr. Polite.

"Sheila who?"

"Sheila, your girlfriend," I suggested.

"Don't know her."

Joey Weber had related little about Sheila other than the fact that she was beautiful, blond, in her mid-twenties, liked emeralds and had a figure that brought traffic to a screeching halt. Charlie repeated this description.

"I said I didn't know her, didn't I?" Petey made a motion to the bartender to give him another margarita.

The bartender was one of these guys who I had seen around for years and maybe talked to twenty times. His name was either Bill or Bob, a skinny guy who freelanced as a blackjack dealer.

"I think you've had enough, Petey."

With a rather graceful gesture, Petey cupped his glass and cocked it back behind his head. The bartender ducked. Just as neatly, Charlie plucked the glass from Petey's hand so that when Petey flung his arm forward, the hand was empty. "Awww," said Petey.

"Get him outta here," said Bob or Bill.

Charlie and I both grabbed an elbow and helped Petey to the exit. He wore black cowboy boots and they swung back and forth about six inches off the floor. Someone opened the door and in no time, we were out on the street. It was snowing again.

"My office," said Charlie, and we turned up the hill.

All this had taken Petey by surprise and in any case his reactions were a trifle fogged over so we had already crossed Putnam and were on our way up the hill when he glanced around, found himself taller than usual and said, "Hey, what gives?"

"I thought we'd have a private drink at my place," said Charlie.

"At least let me fucking walk," said Petey.

Five minutes later Petey was slouched in Charlie's visitor's chair and Charlie was pouring him a shot of Jack Daniel's from the office bottle.

Petey was staring at the picture of Jesse James that hangs on the wall behind Charlie's desk. "Who's that," he said, "your old man?"

"Jesse James."

Petey nodded sagaciously. "I saw the movie." He seemed to have forgotten that Charlie had asked about Sheila. He leaned back comfortably with his short legs stretched out in front of him. His boots barely touched the floor.

Charlie abruptly laughed. "Ha, ha, ha. Sheila told me a good joke the other day."

"That dumb broad," said Petey, "if she told you a joke worth two yuks it'd be a first for sure."

"She still in the same place?" asked Charlie.

"Nah, she moved." A glimmer of intelligence appeared in Petey's eye. "Hey, you're pulling a fast one."

"So where does she live now?" asked Charlie.

Petey got to his feet and swayed back and forth. "I'm outta here," he said.

Charlie held up the bottle of Jack Daniel's. "Nightcap?"

Petey gripped his glass and cocked his arm behind his head. This time I was the one to pluck the glass from his hand. Petey sat back down again. Actually, it was more of a fall. "You know," he said, "that broad loves me. I just can't figure it."

"Maybe it's your brown eyes," I suggested.

Charlie gave me a sharp look, then he sighed. "She could be in a lot of trouble," he said.

"Ha," said Petey, "the cops couldn't touch her."

"I don't mean the cops. Do you know two big guys, always joking?" Charlie described Stubble and his rough pal. I could see Petey try and sit a little straighter in his chair. "It's terrible," said Charlie, "how a simple mistake can get a person killed. Those emeralds that Joey gave her, where do you think the money came from?"

Petey didn't sober up, but he grew alert, the best we could hope for in the circumstances.

"She likes emeralds," said Petey.

"Put that in past tense," I said, "and you could carve it on her tombstone."

"The thing is," said Charlie, "that these misunderstandings could be easily explained. There's no reason she should end up in the trunk of a car. It would be sad if those two guys reached her before we did. After all, I only want to say a few words."

"They'd leave the car at the airport," said Petey. "That's how they like to do it." He started to pour himself some more Jack, then thought better of it.

"So where'd she move to?" asked Charlie.

It shouldn't be thought that Petey rolled over right away, but Charlie had some more words in him of a gentle cautionary nature and at last they popped Petey open like a good knife pops an oyster. Sheila had rented a couple of rooms in Scotia, just west of Schenectady and right down Route 52.

"Sure we can't give you a ride home?" Charlie asked Petey.

"Need another nightcap," he said.

We helped Petey down the stairs and he disappeared into the snow up toward Broadway, leaving baby cowboy boot prints in the white stuff that had freshly fallen. He didn't wave good-bye.

We retrieved Charlie's Mazda from the lot and I scrunched myself into the front seat. I don't think my body bends like Japanese bodies bend. But there was no way we could take the Mercedes. With its busted rear end, it had no taillights. This fact made me sad, but on the other hand it kept Stubble and his rough pal clearly in my mind, which was fine because I didn't want to forget them. It was hard to think they had mothers someplace. Kid sisters. It was hard to think they had ever been Cub Scouts or had gone to camp.

We stopped at a Subway shop to get some Italians for the drive down. It was past nine o'clock and neither of us had eaten. I got to say it takes a certain skill to drive in a snowstorm while eating an Italian and I wasn't sure that Charlie was up to it.

"You don't want to put this off until tomorrow?" I asked.

"I'd like to get there before Petey Loomis sobers up and gives Sheila a call. And don't forget we're still in trouble over that counterfeit money."

"Too bad we can't just snatch the original tape," I suggested. "Then they'd have nothing on us."

"Louie's got it, remember?" Charlie's mouth was full of sandwich and he mumbled. He was driving with his elbows.

"Still, it might be worth a try."

"Don't even think about it."

"Are you really scared about getting charged with running counterfeit money?"

"I doubt we'd go to jail but it would cost me my license. Novak's dying to take it away from me."

"What would you do if that happened?"

Charlie took another bite, chewed thoughtfully, then swallowed. "I'm not sure. Probably leave town."

This surprised me. "What about Janey?"

"She thought if I moved in from the lake, it would solve a lot of problems. Well, I moved and there're still problems. She wants us to see a marriage counselor."

"But you're not even married, for Pete's sake."

"That's one of the problems."

I thought about human relationships. They were like buying a nice pair of shoes that don't exactly fit so you try to accommodate yourself. Then the blisters get busy. For instance, there was the Queen of Softness in her country chalet. Was the guy in the Dodge right now paying her a call? The thing about jealousy was that it kept the big subjects always on the mind: betrayal, loss, revenge. During the course of a normal day, I might remember Rosemary half a dozen times with affection, maybe less, maybe more. But now the thought of her was with me every minute like having an ice cube in my Jockey shorts. I pictured the doofus in the Dodge hefting Rosemary's vast pink breasts with greasy car mechanic fingers and leaving black smudges on the places I had kissed. It was awful.

Charlie managed to eat his Italian and drive through the snow without wrapping us around a flagpole and we got down to Scotia around ten thirty. Then it took twenty minutes to find Sheila's apartment, an old three-story brick building on a residential street. The parked cars all had a layer of snow and most folks were asleep. We slogged through the pristine flakes to the apartment house. Maybe four inches had fallen. On the building directory Sheila was listed as Sheila Pavic. The entrance door was locked. Charlie pushed the button next to her name and we waited. He pushed the button again.

"Yes?" came a voice. It was both sultry and impatient.

"Sheila Pavic?" asked Charlie.

"Who wants to know?"

"My name's Charles Bradshaw. I'd like to talk to you."

"You're outta luck."

"Petey Loomis sent us down."

The voice changed to concern. "Was he drinking?"

"By now he's probably had his fill."

"He promised me he wouldn't," said Sheila.

There wasn't much to be said about that so we waited.

"I guess you'd better come up," she said after another moment.

Sheila's apartment was on the third floor. The stairs creaked and the halls echoed. From behind closed doors came the muted sound of TV chatter. A dog barked once, then yelped. Both Charlie and I were out of breath when we reached her door.

"Fine tough guys we are," I said.

Charlie knocked. Sheila opened up right away.

It is no news to anyone that human couplings are endlessly peculiar, but seeing Sheila brought it home to me once again. She was about six feet one in her socks, which made her about fourteen inches taller than Petey Loomis. Like his nose and her nipples must have been on the same level. And not only was she tall but she was big all over: big breasts, big hips, big shoulders. Even her hair was big, adding about five inches to her height. She was wearing a black satin robe and about the reddest lipstick I had ever seen in my life. It was caked on so thick that even her lips seemed tall. I thought of Joey Weber buying Sheila emeralds. Earlier it had seemed a silly thing. Now I couldn't blame him.

"Hi," said Sheila. "I'm Sheila."

Charlie showed her his ID. I was trying to catch my breath. I mean, even looking at Sheila was like running up three flights of stairs.

"An investigator," said Sheila. She said it slowly, separating all the syllables: in-ves-tig-a-tor. "I thought you were friends of Petey's."

"We just kept him out of jail," I said. "We're probably about the best friends he's got."

"Was he about to throw a glass?"

Charlie and I nodded. Charlie took off his hat.

"He does that," said Sheila, matter-of-factly. "Don't just stand in the hall." She stood back to let us enter. I had to suck in my gut not to brush against her breasts. Being near them was like being in the presence of the Eiffel Tower: it was hard not to look.

Sheila's living room was furnished with a TV and eight big cushions on the floor. Nothing else. The cushions were all covered in different drapery fabric.

"I just moved in," said Sheila. "I'd offer you a drink but I don't keep liquor in the house, because of Petey, you know. Maybe there's some orange juice. Do you like water?"

"That's okay," said Charlie, looking around while trying not to appear that he was looking around.

Sheila sat down gracefully on a cushion. "Have a seat."

Charlie and I squatted down on a couple of cushions. I could hear my knees protesting every inch of the way. Somehow the time had come and gone when I could sit happily on a cushion. I felt like I was expected to lay an egg. Once I was situated I looked up and saw that Sheila was offering me a small green dish.

"Licorice?" she said.

I refused but Charlie took one.

"I love licorice," said Sheila.

I could think of no snappy rejoinder to that remark.

"Have you known Petey long?" asked Sheila.

"Not long," said Charlie. "I wouldn't say long. Actually, I wanted to ask you a few questions about Joey Weber."

Sheila reached up and closed the top of her bathrobe at the neck. "You tricked me," she said.

"What was your interest in Joey?" asked Charlie.

Sheila put a licorice in her mouth. "I don't want to talk about him."

I was sitting there mum as a clam. It occurred to me that the Queen of Softness had probably looked very much like Sheila thirty years earlier. It made me stare at Sheila as if I was reading the story of Rosemary's life. I mean, I had never thought of Rosemary as being anything except what she was: big, busty and fifty-something. But obviously she must have been Sheila's age at some point in her life. And she must have been just as beautiful, if not quite as tall. Then it occurred to me that there was probably not a square centimeter of Rosemary's flesh that some guy hadn't put his lips to. Like she had been toured like Central Park has been toured. She had been traipsed as much as Fifth Avenue. These were new thoughts for me and I found the presence of the thoughts even more startling than the subject of the thoughts, if you see what I mean. I realized I was getting possessive. Me, the beef torpedo, who had prowled the female ocean like a U-boat sinking lady-flotillas. In the past, if I had a problem with a female of my choosing, I would simply sail away. But now I'd gotten myself caught up on the barrier reefs of deep emotion. I'd been beached on the rocky coast of Amour.

Charlie and Sheila were talking.

"What I want to know," said Charlie, "is who pointed you in Joey's direction."

"Nobody did," said Sheila. "We just met, that's all."

"I don't believe it," said Charlie, patiently. "Someone told you to go after him and someone told you to get him to spend money on you."

"A Venus trap," I said, growing alert. "And this is Venus herself."

Sheila looked at me as if I had said something dirty. She still held her robe closed at the neck. On three of her fingers I could see rings with green stones flashing. I wondered if those were emeralds that Joey had sprung for.

"Basically," said Charlie, "you were hired to get Joey into serious debt."

Sheila grew indignant and sat up straight on her cushion. "Nobody paid me money to do anything."

"Then they offered something else," said Charlie. "Did it have to do with Petey Loomis?"

Sheila made a little jump. "Who told you that?"

"Maybe Petey did."

"I never said anything to him about it. He would have gotten too angry. He's proud. Little guys are always proud. I bet if you found a man who was two feet tall, he would be the proudest guy in the world."

Charlie nodded solemnly. He sat with his legs crossed. His corduroy trousers were pulled up, exposing his yellow socks and his knobby shins. His hands were folded in his lap. He looked like a rudimentary Buddha.

"They said they would get him mounts, didn't they," said Charlie. "Louie and whoever else. They said that if you wrapped up Joey Weber for them, they'd let Petey ride."

Sheila's eyes got a little watery. "Petey wasn't getting any mounts at all," said Sheila. "If he doesn't ride, then he drinks, and if he drinks, then he doesn't get mounts. He's already got a bad reputation. But if he had another chance, then he'd pull out of it. I know he would. He loves riding. It's his whole life."

"So you got Joey Weber to spend money on you. Did you have to turn over the stuff he bought?"

Sheila slid one hand over the other, covering her emeralds. "All but a few little things."

"I'm surprised they let you keep anything," said Charlie. "Tell me about Louie. He must be a character."

But Sheila had enough or maybe she was too scared. "I

should never have let you in here," she said. "I'm already in deep trouble."

"Did Louie threaten Joey Weber?"

Sheila abruptly stood up. Her feet were bare and her toenails were the same bright red as her lipstick. Looking up at her from floor level was like staring up at a gorgeous alp. All I wanted was a pickaxe and a rope.

"You got to go," she said.

Charlie tried a few other tactics. Didn't she realize this was a criminal matter? What if the police learned about her involvement? Didn't she know she could go to jail? Didn't she know Petey could be barred from racing forever? But Sheila had been pushed as far as she could be pushed. Although what Charlie was saying put a fright into her, something else frightened her more. I found myself thinking of Stubble and his rough pal.

"Out," said Sheila. "I want you out of here now."

A couple of minutes later Charlie and I were outside on the sidewalk walking toward the Mazda. The snow had stopped and I noticed a couple of stars. Charlie had gotten Sheila to take one of his cards but she hadn't said anything else except, "Leave, go, amscray."

"You were pretty quiet in there," said Charlie, unlocking his car.

"She reminded me of a young Queen of Softness. It sort of left me nonplussed."

Charlie started the car and checked his rearview mirror. "I never thought you'd get delicate on me, Victor."

"Maybe I'm getting knocked down by my own second childhood," I suggested.

Charlie made his way back to Route 52. It was nearly midnight and there wasn't much traffic. Now and then we'd pass a snowplow with its yellow flashing light coloring the landscape.

"So we going to call it a night?" I asked.

"I want to find out more about this Louie character," said Charlie. "And I know a guy who I think can tell me."

"Drop me off at my place," I said. "I need my beauty sleep. Can you imagine Petey in bed with that woman? She must outweigh him by a hundred pounds."

"I was trying not to think about it."

"Jonah fucking the whale," I said.

Charlie dropped me off at my place around quarter past twelve. I considered going upstairs, then instead I went around back to where the Mercedes was parked. I was taking a chance about being stopped since my taillights were all busted up, but I didn't care. That in itself will tell you how far gone I was.

I took a few side streets to get to the edge of town, then I got onto Route 29 and headed toward Schuylerville and Rosemary's. I drove fast and it was twelve thirty when I got to her place. The lights were out. A piece of quarter moon shone off her windows. The fresh snow glistened.

The good news was that the Dodge was no place in evidence. The bad news was that Rosemary's Crown Victoria was gone as well. The new-fallen snow was virginal. No one had come or gone since early in the evening.

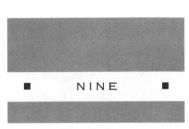

■ NINE ■

After Charlie dropped me off he also took a drive on Route 29 out of Saratoga but he went west rather than east. He was going to see George Marotta, who had a fancy restaurant up in the hills. Charlie didn't worry about getting Marotta out of bed. Since Marotta had had his stroke, he hardly slept two hours a night. It used to be that Charlie would see Marotta almost every day in the YMCA pool, but all that was in the past. Charlie still swam but Marotta hadn't been in the pool for six years. Occasionally Charlie would see him downtown in his wheelchair or being driven in his Ford van. Marotta was about ten years older than Charlie, and Charlie used to complain that Marotta passed him in the pool again and again. He even gave Charlie tips on how to improve his stroke. Not any more. Good stroke, bad stroke was how I saw it.

The restaurant was five miles out of town on a road with some dairy farms. Outside of racing season it tended to get few customers, which led some people to think that Marotta kept it open for reasons other than dishing out big plates of lasagna. Over the years at least fifty people had told me that Marotta laundered money for downstate racketeers. Maybe it was true, maybe not—Marotta had never confided in me, but Charlie knew that Marotta counted a truckload of racketeers among his summertime customers, which was why he was paying him a midnight visit. He figured that Marotta could tell him about Louie.

The restaurant was a long yellow building at the end of a parking lot. There was more snow in the hills and the lot was surrounded by small white mountains of bulldozed snow, giving it an alpine aspect. A Ford van and two cars were parked near the entrance. The snow in the lot was five inches deep and smooth as a bedsheet, which indicated neither customers nor traffic. Charlie stuck his Mazda beside the other cars and got out. He was wearing galoshes. Charlie always wears galoshes if there is more than an eighth of an inch of snow. On either side of the front door of the restaurant were Roman pillars, which during the summer were linked by grapevines.

The restaurant didn't seem exactly open but neither did it seem closed. At least the front door was unlocked and a light was burning above it. Charlie entered and stamped his galoshes on the mat, then passed through the foyer into the restaurant. The Roman motif was continued inside with a wall mural of the Colosseum and a bunch of curly-headed plaster statues with the noses and arms missing, which I guess was how they had been made: already busted. And pillars, lots of Roman pillars with bunches of red plastic grapes hanging from their capitals. Ten tables with red tablecloths and red teardrop candles were grouped around the bar to form a small intimate restaurant. Beyond that was an open space not so much like a dance floor as like a football field. On the far side of the open space were stacks of extra tables and chairs piled right to the ceiling.

Four men were watching horse races on television. One of the men was in a wheelchair, and Charlie knew it was Marotta. The sound had been turned off. As Charlie approached he saw a bunch of tiny horses break from the gate. A young man sitting at the bar made a note on a piece of yellow paper. The bartender and a waiter in a black jacket watched with their arms folded. The faces of all four were illuminated by the screen. Marotta's wheelchair was directly beneath the TV. No one spoke. Charlie stopped to wait until the race was over.

"Dogmeat, dogmeat," said the young man at the bar.

"The number five horse isn't bad," said Marotta.

"That's because the others are terrible." The young man glanced around and saw Charlie. "Hey, we're closed."

The number five horse crossed the finish line about four lengths ahead of the nearest challenger.

"I wanted a few words with George," said Charlie, crossing the rest of the room.

Marotta turned his chair. "The swimming gumshoe," he said. His voice was slurred but it wasn't from drinking. The left side of Marotta's mouth was turned down and his left eye was drooping. He was a thin man with curly gray hair and a small bump in the middle of his nose where it had been broken years before.

"Shall I throw him out?" said the young man.

"You got any better entertainment for me?" asked Marotta. "This is the first fresh face I've seen all week." He held his hand out toward Charlie. "I suppose you've got favors to ask."

"That's true enough," said Charlie, taking his hand, "but it's good to see you anyway."

"I'm three-quarters dead," said Marotta, "and what's left are just gripes and complaints. You want something to drink?"

"A beer would be okay."

"Two Heinekens," said Marotta to the bartender. "Push me over to that far table so we can talk without these creeps trying to overhear. We're so bored that we listen to the rats chatter."

"You'll get busy this summer," said Charlie.

"With any luck I'll be dead by the summer."

Charlie pushed him over to a table. The young man at the bar watched them, then turned away to the TV.

"That's my nephew, Alphie. He stands to inherit. The lucky stiff." Marotta laughed, then began to cough.

Charlie sat down and put his hat on the table. He started to speak, then stopped as he saw the waiter approaching with two Heinekens. The waiter poured the beer.

"You want the candle lit?" asked the waiter. He was a thin balding man about the same age as Marotta.

"Fuck the candle," said Marotta.

The waiter already had his matches out. "It'll make it cheerier."

"Okay, okay, light the candle," said Marotta.

The waiter lit the candle, then departed.

"I'm surrounded by people who try to make me happy," said Marotta. "It's depressing. You still swimming?"

"Not as often as I'd like."

"My health insurance paid for a whirlpool bath. That's the only water I get."

"Things change," said Charlie.

Marotta reached out for his glass. "But not for the better." He took a drink, holding the glass to the right side of his mouth. "So what's on your mind?"

"I need to know about a man called Louie who wants to smuggle counterfeit hundred-dollar bills out of Montreal."

"You got a scary way of jumping right to the point," said Marotta. "I shouldn't even be talking to you."

"It's a little late for that."

"These are professional operators you want to know about."

Charlie waited. Marotta took another drink of beer and rolled it around in his mouth as if it didn't taste right to him.

"Louie's name is really Luigi but he likes to be called Louie: Louie Angel, formerly Luigi Anzilotti. He wouldn't like me talking to you. But what's he going to do? Kill me?" Marotta laughed, then began to cough again. He fished a cigarette out of his shirt pocket and lit it. "How'd you get mixed up with this?"

"Do you know Felix Weber?"

"The money man."

So Charlie told Marotta how old man Weber had picked me up in the Parting Glass and made a patsy out of me, how I'd paid Eddie Gillespie to go up to Montreal and how Eddie had mopped the floor—make that the parking lot—with Joey Weber. Then how Charlie and I had gone up to Montreal together to get the counterfeit money not knowing it was counterfeit money. And he told about the videotape and the two hooligans who had busted up my apartment and busted up the Mercedes as well.

"Louie Angel," said Charlie, "hired Sheila Pavic to rope in old man Weber's son, Joey. Joey stole money that was basically Louie's money in order to buy Sheila presents, and old man Weber had to figure out a way to get it back. So he decided to rob himself and he hired Victor as his courier because he thought Victor would be easy to rob. Anyway, Victor is now on videotape picking up the suitcase in Montreal and I'm involved as well. Weber claims that Louie has done all this in order to get him active in smuggling counterfeit money."

"And what do you think?"

"I think if Louie wanted to smuggle money from Montreal, he could find a hundred ways of doing it without using Weber, so he must want Weber for something else."

Marotta lifted his right hand and smoothed back his gray hair with the middle two fingers. "The counterfeit money is nothing. It's just the hook. I bet Louie wants Weber's entire business. Weber's got money contacts all over the world. The money-laundering potential of such an operation is enormous."

"Weber said that Louie was already helping him out, fronting him money when he needed it in a hurry."

"Louie wasn't doing it to be nice," said Marotta. "He don't know where nice's at. He gave up being nice when he got born."

Charlie drank some of his beer. Over by the bar the other three men were still watching horse races. "My own problem is simple," said Charlie. "I've got an acting police chief in Saratoga who is eager to take away my license. This business would give him the perfect excuse. So I guess I want to know more about Louie Angel."

"Louie's a punk. He came up to Albany from the city eight or nine years ago. He's got no respect for how stuff gets done. What they call organized crime, it's run like the army. You always got somebody over you, right to the top. Louie's trouble is he thinks he can operate independently. Over the years he's taken over some other guys' operations. He's brought in more dough and a few of the bosses downstate like him. But he's ambitious. Give him a plain Hershey bar and he wants nuts. Give him nuts and he wants a banana. Anything he gets, he wants something bigger. That's not so easy."

"You mean because of the police?"

"Not necessarily. You got a whole network of operations working throughout the East. Everybody gets a nice piece of pie. They stay out of the papers, don't attract attention, a few cops get their cut. Business moves along like a well-ordered machine. It's like equilibrium. Then Louie comes along. Some of the guys he took orders from weren't too young anymore and after a year or two Louie rolled right over them. And he must have said to himself, I got this with no trouble, maybe I can get some more. And what happens to your equilibrium? It gets fucked, that's what. If Louie gets a bigger cut, then someone else gets a smaller cut. That's what it amounts to. People get unhappy and when that happens they start attracting attention. They get mad. They start pushing and shoving. Before you know it the cops are looking around. Then the Feds."

"So what does this have to do with Weber?"

"If Louie Angel takes over Weber's operation, then his money is absolutely out of here. No one will know how much he's making or what he's doing. And this counterfeit money, it's Chinese. Those guys don't care about how things get done over here. They got no respect for U.S. methods. It lets Louie Angel completely bypass the normal channels of operation. It lets him move to the top without passing Go."

"What do you care about any of this?" asked Charlie.

Marotta laughed, then coughed again. He took another drink of beer and wiped his mouth with a white handkerchief. "I'm like a Republican. I don't like change. But it's more than that. If Louie gets people mad, it will lead to unpleasantness and people getting taken out, which means newspapers and TV get involved, which means the cops. The nice thing about equilibrium is that it lets everything remain sleepy. But once it gets broken it's an absolute bitch to put back together again. What you say about Louie Angel and old man Weber, all that is news to me but it doesn't surprise me. As I say, Louie's ambitious. Maybe he can control Weber and everything will stay quiet. But can he control your friend Victor? Is he really going to let him drive back and forth to Montreal?"

I got to interrupt and say that when Charlie repeated this to me, I felt a burst of pride. Nobody can push around Vic Plotz, that's what I thought. I got ways of getting revenge that would make the Borgia family cringe. But Marotta was praising neither my keen intelligence nor my valiant heart. In fact, praise never came into it.

"Plotz is a fuckup," said Marotta. "He's got no rules. You don't know what he's going to do next."

Charlie didn't say how he responded to this. He drew a dark veil over that part of the conversation. I got to mention that about a dozen years ago, when I was working for Charlie, Marotta's wife hired me to tail him around. She thought Marotta had found himself a girlfriend and he was squeezing her on the side, which turned out not to be the case. But perhaps I was not as subtle as I might have been. In those years I was just a beginner in the detective trade and perhaps I made a few mistakes, a few faux pas, partly because I had Eddie Gillespie helping me. Actually, they were more Eddie's faux pas than mine. Sad to say, these were mistakes that Marotta has never forgiven me for, which was no doubt what led him to speak ill of me on this occasion. As for Marotta's devoted wife, she ditched him shortly after he had his stroke. I tried to tell him at the time that she was nothing but trouble, but he didn't listen and his life went sour. Now he was still angry about it.

Charlie left Marotta's restaurant shortly after one in the morning and drove back to Janey's. He had no particular plans except wanting to extricate himself, and me too, from Weber's problems with Louie Angel. If he could help Weber, then he was glad to, but what bothered Charlie in particular were Louie Angel's methods.

"These goons he's got working for him," Marotta had said, "Steel and Clover. They sound like a fucking law firm. Two big guys. I don't know where Louie Angel found them, maybe out west. The point is they're not from around here and none of their loyalties are based around here. The East means nothing to them. Talk about equilibrium, Steel and Clover don't know the meaning of the word. No loyalty, no sense of tradition, they only want to make their money fast and get out. Louie Angel thinks he runs them, but guys like that, no one runs them. The only good thing is that they tend to be short-lived. Nobody finally wants them around and they end up in their car trunk."

I wouldn't say Charlie scared easily, at least I've never seen him scared for himself. But his life had changed. He was no longer living on his own in a little cottage on Lake Saratoga. He was living with Janey Burris and her three daughters, who were eighteen, sixteen and fourteen. Pretty creatures every one. The oldest one was waiting to hear from colleges and would be gone in the fall. The other two would be entering ninth and eleventh grades. Charlie thought of Steel and Clover barging into Janey's house. He thought of their cheerful violent faces as he had seen them through the rear window of my Mercedes. So the difficulty from his standpoint was to extricate himself from Louie Angel, while also avoiding Steel and Clover. And maybe that would have been possible if I hadn't made a mess of things.

When Charlie reached Janey's house, Janey was still awake, playing solitaire at the kitchen table and sipping whiskey. She wore a blue bathrobe of Charlie's that hid her small body. "When the first card facing up is a queen, I always lose. What do you think about that?"

"Cheat," said Charlie.

She tilted her head at him like a bird. "You're looking somber."

"I'm feeling somber."

"Like a little Jim Beam?"

"Not tonight."

"You must be very somber indeed."

Charlie wanted to tell her about Louie Angel, Felix Weber and the rest of it, but he didn't want to frighten her. Janey wouldn't be frightened for herself. She too would be worried about the girls, but she would be also worried about Charlie. As he looked at her smiling at him, he again told himself that he should never have moved into Saratoga from the lake. No matter how much he loved her, he felt himself dangerous in the same way that Typhoid Mary had been dangerous.

He said to me later, "I've got people going back thirty years who have a grudge against me. These guys, Steel and Clover, they're just the newest versions. I should get out of this whole racket. I should go off into the mountains and live by myself. I should be a monk."

"That doesn't sound like fun," I told him.

"Sometimes fun is too expensive. If I went off by myself, at least it would be safe and I wouldn't get anyone in trouble."

"You make safety sound too expensive."

"Maybe so," Charlie told me, but he didn't look as if he agreed.

But with Janey he didn't say much of anything. Charlie sat down at the kitchen table and glanced at her cards. He felt tired and wanted to go to bed. "You can move the ten of hearts."

Janey smiled at him. "I'm still exploring my options. Where have you been?"

"Talking to an old friend."

"You don't want to tell me about it?"

"I'm afraid of getting you involved."

Janey stretched out a hand and put it over one of Charlie's. "I'm already involved."

"That's what worries me."

"Even if you lived out at the lake I'd be involved. I want you here where I can keep an eye on you."

"Are the girls asleep?"

"I hope so. They've got school tomorrow."

"And everything's okay with them?"

"Apart from fighting over who gets to use the telephone."

"Maybe I'll have some whiskey after all," said Charlie.

"That's what I like to hear," said Janey. She gathered the cards together and got to her feet. "Ice?"

■ TEN ■

Steel and Clover: I didn't as yet know that was how they were called when I saw them the first thing Thursday morning. Their names came later like the credits at the end of a movie. It was nine o'clock and I was on my way over to Charlie's office to find out what he had learned from Marotta the night before. I was taking the Mercedes. That was a mistake. I should have left the Mercedes where it would be safe, like in a bank. I should have walked. But it was raining a cold March rain and I didn't want to get wet. What's a little wetness to a busted automobile, that's what I want to know. Absolutely zilch.

My apartment in the Algonquin on Broadway is shabby but nice, just as I like it. Behind the back is a parking lot where I dock the Mercedes and where it seems happy, musing with the lesser automobiles. Maybe because I hadn't had a lot of sleep, I was less alert than usual. I lacked the tippy-toes of attentiveness. The fact

that the Queen of Softness had not been home the previous midnight had given a kind of indigestion to my dreams, meaning it
had been a rocky night with lots of mental flatulence. But maybe
that's just an excuse. Maybe I just wasn't paying attention.

So I pulled out of the parking lot and my wipers were going
whap-whap and I was just clicking my seat belt into place and
getting to the street when, whambang, something smacks into
me head-on and I hear the tinkle of my headlights dribbling onto
the sidewalk and I'm tossed forward against the straps. I look out
through the rain and there is this big Chevy Blazer jammed in
front of me and in the front seat are these two guys—Steel and
Clover—whose names I don't know yet and they are waving and
smiling and blowing me kisses. Looking at them, you would think
they were the happiest guys on this shiny green planet, guys you
would be glad to know if they had not just smashed the front end
of your Mercedes.

So I put the Mercedes in reverse, back up about five feet and
stop. Like I meant to inspect the damage, which was perhaps
dumb of me, because the Blazer leaps forward again and for the
second time bashes my front end and I am bounced up and hit my
head on the roof. Once more I hear hardware and bits of glass
hit the pavement. Once more I look up to see Steel and Clover
laughing and blowing me kisses.

Well, there was a rear exit out of the parking lot onto Maple
and I took it and my back wheels were spinning fast and I was
throwing up a lot of mud. But once out on the street, I saw that
the Blazer hadn't followed me. A few quick bashes was all they
wanted, a couple of pokes in the nose. So I drove over to Phila
Street to Charlie's office and on the way I heard little clinks and
tinkles as bits of my front end decanted onto the pavement. And
after I had parked in the lot next to Charlie's Mazda, I did a quick
inspection. Both headlights, the parking lights and the fog lights
were busted. The bumper had lost its streamlined shape and the
grill had a chewed look. The noble hood ornament was skewed.
In fact, the front end of the Mercedes now resembled the rear end

of the Mercedes. Both had a junkyard aspect, a ripped and tat-
tered cast. I rarely cry and I did not cry then, but I felt like I
should.

I made my way up Phila to Charlie's office and though it was
still raining, I hardly paid attention. What was exterior wetness
compared to a busted Mercedes? I had a wetness in my soul.
There were about twenty wooden stairs up to the second floor
and every single one of them creaked like the scary sounds in a
fun house. Charlie, unfortunately, was in a chipper mood.

"No coffee and doughnuts?" he asked, looking up from some
papers.

"I got attacked again," I said. I took off my raincoat and
shook it.

"Attacked?"

"Those two cheerful guys, Stubble and his rough pal, they
bashed the front end of my Mercedes."

"Steel and Clover," said Charlie.

And that was how I learned their names.

I got to say that Charlie was a good friend, whatever other
shortcomings he might have. He called out to Bruehegger's for
bagels and coffee and he didn't make any more little jokes.

"Have you ever heard of a mafioso by the name of Louie Angel or Luigi Anzilotti?" he asked as we were waiting for our grub.

"No. Is that the same Louie who's got his hooks into Felix
Weber?"

So Charlie told me about his late-night conversation with
George Marotta and I have to confess that I heard nothing to
cheer me up. I had a bad case of the jitters and when the kid from
Bruehegger's thumped on the door, I elevated several inches out
of my chair and felt little white mice doing cartwheels along my
spine. But a cinnamon raisin bagel is a powerful restorative and as
I worked on my second I began to wonder how I might wiggle out
of my troubles.

"But what does Louie Angel want from me?" I asked.

"I suspect he wants to use you as a courier and he's told Steel
and Clover to soften you up."

"How could I be a courier? I'm not a tough guy."

"That's what he wants. Put you in the right clothes and cut your frizzy hair and he could have you looking like an absolute cream puff, the kind of guy who could be trusted with anything. You'd carry the money through customs and Steel and Clover would be nearby to see that everything went well."

"And to make sure that I behaved."

"Exactly. Both you and Weber would be as tame as kittens."

"Thanks," I said. "And what about you? You're on that tape as well."

"I could be doing the same thing. I mean, as far as they're concerned, I'm an accident. They never expected me to be there. Maybe they just want to frighten me away. I expect we'll soon find out."

"And this is all because Louie's got a simple little videotape and the services of Steel and Clover?"

"That's about it."

"Where does Louie live?"

"Why do you want to know?"

"Maybe I want to send him a thank-you note."

"Victor, the only way we can get out of this in one piece is to stay quiet and maybe put some pressure on Louie Angel from another direction. Marotta says that Louie is none too popular with his criminal associates. Possibly something can be done there. As for you, you should just go home and keep your door locked until I call."

But that was not the way I saw it.

About ten thirty I left Charlie's office and drove out to see the Queen of Softness. It was still raining. New York State has a law that says you got to have your headlights on when your windshield wipers are in operation, which is the kind of law that gets bureaucrats their retirement Timexes. Anyway, since my headlights had been turned into dimples by Steel and Clover, I had to sneak out of town by back roads and hope that no copper pulled me over. I got to say I felt sad about the Mercedes. For several years I'd been stuck driving little cars while I saved up my pennies.

Even though the Mercedes had two hundred big ones on the odometer, it was still a Mercedes. And even though it was a mustard-colored 230 four-door, it still had the hum, the ride, the style. And now it also had a bashed front and rear end.

In my devious brain I was developing the inklings of a plan that would free us from Louie Angel, but it needed further cogitation. Someplace Louie had the original video showing me picking up the money. If he lost it, then what muscle would he have? Threats and brawn, that was all. Such were my thoughts. But I was also thinking of Eddie Gillespie, his turban and his white pajamas. Surely an outfit like that could come in useful.

The Queen of Softness was on her throne behind the cash register when I strolled through the door. Henrietta was slinging plates behind the counter to hungry truckers and old Ernie Boner was cracking eggs in the kitchen. The parking lot was free of the offensive Dodge, and Rosemary's Crown Victoria was parked in its usual spot in front of her prefab ranch house just where I liked to see it. Although I had recently eaten several bagels, I decided that a bran muffin and a cup of Postum would go down comfortably.

I kissed Rosemary on the cheek, then fought off a sneeze as a bit of her powder wafted up my nose.

"How's my big fellow?" she said. She was wearing her orange leopard-spot blouse with spots that glowed in the dark.

"I am the very acme of contentment," I said. Having made a small lie, I made another. "Were you out last night? I gave you a call but I got no answer."

Rosemary raised her sculpted eyebrows. "When was that?"

"Around eleven," I lied again.

She smiled. "That was when I was in the hot tub."

"Then I called again around twelve to say goodnight."

"Would you believe I actually went to sleep in the hot tub. I was lucky I didn't drown."

"Awful thought," I said with a smile. But deep inside it was all weeping and gnashing of teeth. Rosemary was lying to me. She had been out. Her car had been gone. She had been with the guy in the Dodge. For a moment I considered taking the Queen of Softness by the throat and shaking her like a golden retriever shakes a squirrel. Then I felt shocked by my feelings: in itself a first. But I knew it wasn't me, it was the jealousy.

"You look a trifle fatigued," said Rosemary. "How about a big bowl of hot bran?"

"I can't stop," I said. "I was just driving by and thought I'd say howdy." The very words burned in my mouth. How could she look at me so benignly? She must have the heart of a demon. "I got to go." I headed for the door.

"But when will I see you?" Rosemary called after me.

"When you see me!" I shouted. Then I was gone.

I drove back to Saratoga in a fog: both mental and physical. The thought of the Queen of Softness being poked by strangers in the night sent the steam whistling from my ears and miniature porcupines surging through my Jockey shorts. This was the woman to whom I had pledged my later years, whose soft white belly so nearly matched my own white belly. What could she see in this other guy? What did he have that I didn't? Then one word popped into my dome: stamina. What he lacked in softness, he made up for in beef and vigor. I liked to drowse off around two in the morning and that was probably my fatal mistake. This guy in the Dodge, most likely a youngster, at two in the morning he was just getting warmed up. I would have to change my life. I would have to eat bean sprouts and drink carrot juice. I'd have to diet.

These were the thoughts that attacked my brain as I drove into town. I imagined myself swimming side by side with Charlie at the Y. Maybe I'd become one of those old farts who wore a girdle and put spots of ruby red on their cheeks. I might even have to dye my hair. I was coming in on Union Avenue past the racetrack and the Racing Hall of Fame. The rain had gotten harder. Up ahead of me the light changed at Nelson and I drew to a stop. Union dead-ends at Congress Park, and in the few blocks between were the big houses and redbrick buildings that used to make up Skidmore College. I sat at the light and thought about my waistline. What was I? Forty-two? Forty-four? Would the Queen of Softness swear to be mine if I cut down to thirty-six, even thirty-eight?

Suddenly there was a crash and I was thrown against my left door and the Mercedes rose up on two left wheels as something big smashed into me. The light was still red and the Mercedes was shivering all over. Turning, I saw the huge metal grill of the Chevy Blazer. Through its windshield, I saw the cheerful faces of Steel and Clover blowing me kisses. Have you ever wanted to throw yourself on the ground and cry? Instead, I floored the Mercedes through the light, then made a quick left onto Clark Street. Looking into the rearview mirror, I saw I wasn't being followed. There was a whining noise as part of the right front fender rubbed against the tire. I pulled to the curb and got out. The whole right side of the Mercedes was bashed with a waffle pattern from the Blazer's big bumper. I yanked back on the fender so it wouldn't rub. Needless to say it was raining and I got wet. I returned to the front seat and did some doleful thinking. Then, with a sigh, I pressed down on the accelerator. I had to pay a visit to old man Weber. As I drove, I could hear bits of the Mercedes sprinkling onto the street. You might think I was sad: I was worse than sad.

Felix Weber talked to me in his garage back behind the house on Court Street. He said his wife had poodles and they could be dangerous. From inside the house I could hear barking. It sounded like twenty or thirty poodles. They made me think of the wild packs of Chihuahuas that used to drag conquistadors from their horses and eat them for snacks. Weber stood by a workbench. He had a straight back for an oldster. His stiff white hair was brushed straight up. His skinny nose made a little up-turned point. He looked like an elderly Woody Woodpecker. He also looked depressed and a trifle jumpy. I wondered about his relationship with Steel and Clover.

"Why d'you want to know where Louie Angel lives?" he asked.

"I feel that if I am to establish a business relationship with him, I should know where he hangs his hat."

"That's not a good enough reason." Arranged in neat little rows on the wall behind Weber were about fifty New York State license plates going back to the 1930s. The mustard-colored ones reminded me of my busted Mercedes.

"Then let's talk about something else," I said. "Did you know that Louie Angel hired Sheila Pavic to throw her wonderful oversized body into the path of your son? Joey didn't meet her accidentally. She snagged him. He was her private tuna. And once she snagged him, then she got him to spend money on her. Then he spent more and more money on her, till he had to swipe money from you. Money that also belonged to Louie Angel. And how were you going to pay back that money? So maybe you think Louie did this in order to make you run some counterfeit money for him. Nah, don't you believe it. Louie's got dozens of guys who could do it. The counterfeit money is just the beginning. He wants your whole operation. He wants a way to peddle his crooked bucks throughout the entire world and get them back squeaky clean. As for you and Joey—you're hardly more than nuisances. And once Mr. Angel has got himself comfortably into your network, then you and Joey are going to be retired. At least that's how I see it and I bet you see it the same way. Are you acquainted with Steel and Clover, those cheerful lads?"

Old man Weber listened without expression or maybe his face had a little more sag in it, a woeful bend in the middle. "This all happened because that guy you hired broke Joey's wrist."

"It would have happened anyway. You think Louie didn't know what your son was up to? I'll bet he's even got a videotape of Joey getting his wrist broke. I bet that's what Steel and Clover find so funny. They're laughing at how Joey got whopped. Louie wanted you, he wanted to get his hooks into you, and he did."

"So why do you want his address?"

"Because he's got his hooks into me as well and maybe I can think of a way to get free. And if I get free, then you get free.

What's the harm? He's already got you caught like a pooch in a net. Even if my plan fails, you won't be any worse off than you are now."

"What's your plan?"

"That's my secret."

Eventually old man Weber gave me the address. He didn't seem like a happy guy and if I had been him, I would have taken the wife and all those poodles down to Costa Rica for a long vacation. Best to jump ship when the jumping was good, but of course he was worried about Joey, the watermelon of his eye.

After leaving Weber, I took the Mercedes over to a body shop I knew and left it. It was obvious that if I kept driving it, then Steel and Clover would bash up the left side as well. Then they would start on the roof. Then the soft underbelly. It was time to bring this automotive abuse to a close. Presumably, this ordeal with Louie's henchmen would at last come to an end and once it was over I could retrieve the Mercedes. In the meantime, I got myself a rental, a little blue Toyota Tercel, and once again I thought how the curves of my corpus magnus must be so unlike the curves on your average Japanese body. Driving that car was like trying to wear ballet slippers: it was a tight fit.

But it ran okay if you like that sewing machine sound and by noon I was driving down to Ballston Spa to visit Eddie Gillespie.

I found him in his turban and his white karate pajamas. He was sitting on the floor in his living room trying to read a book on yoga and Zen meditation. Like his finger was slowly moving across the page and his lips were waggling. When he saw me he stopped reading and raised one index finger.

"Goso say, 'A buffalo passes the window. His head, horns, and four legs all go past. But why can't the tail pass too?' "

I stood in the doorway. "What the fuck are you up to?" From where I stood I could see Eddie's wife messing around in the kitchen. She still wore her turban.

Eddie again raised his finger. "Ummon say, 'The world is vast and wide. Why do you put on your seven-piece robe at the sound of the bell?' "

"I'm going to smack you if you keep this up," I said.

Eddie bowed his head to me. "What's the good of wearing a turban, if you don't take any benefit from the turban? These are Zen koans. They make me seem wise."

"Zen guys don't wear turbans," I said.

"You think anybody in Ballston Spa knows that?"

He had a point. "I suppose they think you're smart talking that crap."

"I impressed the mailman."

"How are you earning your bucks now that you've got lice?"

"Wise man said, 'The money and the hand take two different paths: one to the mountain, one to the valley.' Tell you the truth, I'm broke."

"Would you like to earn a hundred bucks for an hour's work?"

"What would I have to do?"

I tried to look benign and grandfatherly. "No more than you're doing now. By being wise."

"Would I get in trouble?"

"Jesus, Eddie, I hate a suspicious nature. It's perfectly innocent." Maybe I was lying, maybe I wasn't. Just to be safe, I kept my fingers crossed behind my back.

■ ELEVEN ■

One of the things that Eddie Gillespie has in excess is questions. Like he doesn't know when to keep his lip zipped. You would think that the offer of one hundred smackers for one hour's work might also buy his eagerness, goodwill and silence. But no, he needed to interrogate me.

"But why are you wearing a Niagara-Mohawk meter man uniform?" he asked.

"It was handy."

"Are you working for them?"

"Only for today."

"Have they actually given you a job?"

"Not in so many words."

"And where are we going?"

"Colonie, like I said."

It was early in the afternoon and we were driving south on the Northway, a sort of geographical oxymoron. Although the rain had let up, the road was wet and big trucks threw up muddy water onto the windshield of the Tercel. And when the trucks went by the Tercel would shiver and shake. The Mercedes never shivered.

Eddie's white turban was squashed under the roof and he had to slouch in his seat. It gave his body a sullen configuration to go with his sullen expression. "I'm not going to have to do anything that will get anyone mad, will I?"

"Eddie, how could you suggest such a thing?"

"I've been thinking over the stuff I've done with you that has led me to get bruises. I shouldn't come within ten feet of you. You're more dangerous than lice."

"You got that nice money in Montreal, didn't you?"

"I used excessive force. If I hadn't done that, I wouldn't be wearing this turban."

"What's it look like underneath?" I asked, perversely curious.

"Hideous."

"Eddie, we're doing this for Charlie, not for me. Be generous. Look at how he has helped you over the years. He's gotten you jobs; he's kept you out of jail. Do you want him to lose his license?"

"Aww," said Eddie, mollified.

Louie Angel's house in Colonie was a big baby blue ranch house with an attached garage and two pillars out in front of the driveway. On each pillar was a little black iron lion's head. There was a tall pine tree in the yard and black shutters on the windows. The drapery was all drawn. I drove by slowly and saw there was a side door into what looked like a kitchen. A black Mercedes 300E, a new one, was parked in the driveway. Next to it was the Chevy Blazer. I was sorry to see the Blazer. On the other hand, the presence of Steel and Clover would keep me from dawdling. Then it occurred to me that I should just keep on driving, maybe stop someplace nice for lunch, then drive back to Saratoga. But that wouldn't solve the problem of Louie Angel and old man Weber.

But it was more complicated than that; the more nervous I became, the more I thought of the Queen of Softness. Here I was being replaced by a younger man, what were the reasons for this reversal of fortune? Stamina, yes, but what else? Strength, power, courage: it was a long list. To forget Louie Angel and the boys in the Blazer was to give instant credibility to that list of deficiencies. This was no time to argue that discretion was the better part of valor. What was discretion but chickenheartedness and a capitulation to age? If I tweedled back to Saratoga without doing anything, then I might as well kiss Rosemary good-bye. It was even worse than her rejecting me, I would reject myself. So even though I was scared, I had to act. It was either terrifying action or no more sweet, sweet flesh and hot tubs in the night, or at least that was how I saw it.

"That's the house," I told Eddie. I drove another fifty yards and parked.

"Pretty color. I like baby blue."

"It probably matches his eyes."

"Whose eyes?"

"Louie Angel's."

"Probably matches Frank Sinatra's eyes," said Eddie, being difficult. "And what do you want me to do?"

We got out of the car and started walking back. It had begun to drizzle again: not really rain, but wet. Eddie walked very straight. He was about six feet tall and thin. His turban gave another four or five inches to his height. He wore a cream-colored quilted vest and white karate pajamas but without the black belt. On his feet were little black kung fu slippers. And Eddie was calm. He was better calm.

"I want you to knock on the door and when someone answers I want you to say, 'My monkey up you tree.' "

Eddie stopped and turned to face me. "Say that again?"

" 'My monkey up you tree.' Don't change the words or correct the grammar. Just say it. Maybe you can roll the 'r' in 'tree.' Say it slowly with a little accent. If they ask you questions, just repeat what you said. Don't change it. Don't elaborate. Maybe you can point to the pine tree."

"My monkey up you tree," said Eddie.

"That's it. Great. You should be on the stage."

"I don't want to do it."

"A hundred bucks, Eddie, for one line of dialogue. They don't even get that on Broadway."

"My monkey up you tree."

"Perfect. Brando couldn't do it better."

"Make it one fifty."

"No can do, Eddie. This is just a little job."

"Then I'm going home."

"Okay, one fifty."

"My monkey up you tree."

"Perfect."

"And who are these people?"

"Old friends, chums."

"Will they try to hurt me?"

"They'll just laugh. They're good guys."

"And what are you going to do?"

"Me? I'm going to read their meter."

We separated. Eddie walked toward the front door and I walked toward the side door. I figured I had about five minutes in the house if I moved fast. As I approached the side door, I took a small black mustache from my pocket and stuck it on my upper lip. Then I put on a pair of black horn-rimmed glasses with clear lenses. I hadn't wanted Eddie to see the mustache or glasses. They would only rile him up. I wanted to keep him calm. My gray frizzy hair was tucked under my Ni-Mo hat.

I knocked at the door. Through the glass I saw a black lady in a gray uniform lean a mop against the counter, make a "what-now?" face and walk toward me. Just as she opened the door, I heard the front doorbell chime.

"Meterman," I said.

"You was just here the other day," she said.

"A glitch in the system. Gotta do it again."

She sighed as if she was used to glitches in the system, then she stood aside to let me enter. She was a big woman with a pretty face. Maybe she was forty-five.

"You know where it is?" she asked.

"I'm new," I said. "Just got transferred from Cohoes."

She pointed out of the kitchen. "Down that hall, first door on your left, down the cellar stairs and turn right. It's next to the furnace."

"Sure you don't want to do it for me?"

"Get on with you," she said.

I trotted across the kitchen and she picked up the mop. In the hallway, I opened the door to the cellar, stamped once on the cellar stairs, then just kept going down the hall. The open door to the cellar kept the maid from being able to see me. The floor was carpeted. I put an expression on my face that said that I was a crazy lost meter man.

The hall led into a dining room. To the left was the living room and to the right was some kind of den or family room.

From the front door, I could hear voices. Someone was saying, "What's up the tree?"

And someone else, "His monkey. His fucking monkey's up the fucking tree, you deaf?"

And someone else, "What's his fucking monkey doing in my fucking yard?"

I liked that last question. It had a philosophical edge that I appreciated. The living room was a formal place with long pea-green couches and glass-topped coffee tables. It didn't even have a TV. I headed for the den.

"I'm not climbing any fucking tree," I heard someone say. "No fucking way."

"Let me shoot it," said another voice. "Are monkeys protected?"

"You can't shoot his fucking monkey," said a third voice. "It'd get blood on my tree."

The den seemed to be a place where bowling trophies were kept. There were a lot of them. And there were photographs of guys shaking hands and photographs of guys seated at tables with white tablecloths and half-empty glasses grinning up at the camera. No books except phone books. A couple of Barco-Loungers and a little bar with bottles of hootch. A big Toshiba forty-two-inch TV stood against one wall. On top of it were a stack of videotapes, a dozen or more. I started pawing through them. The trouble was that most weren't marked: just plain videotapes in black cases. On the other hand, did I expect to see my name on the label? "Vic Plotz's Trip to Montreal." I took the top three and started to leave.

Then I saw a door next to the TV that was slightly ajar. It looked like a closet but when I opened it I saw it was a small office without windows. There was a safe, some file cabinets, a desk and a computer. I found it touching that crooks were using computers these days and I wondered if you can get e-mail in prison. Also on the desk was a metal attaché case, maybe it was aluminum, about four inches by twelve inches by sixteen inches with a black leather handle. I don't know if I can make this clear, but the box had a tremendous authority about it. It looked important. A strongbox, I said to myself. I picked it up. It had substantial weight, seductive heft. I took it with me.

But as I was coming out of the den into the dining room, I heard a certain commotion at the front door, a shout, then the door slammed and someone shouted, "There's no fucking monkey up that tree!"

Then someone else shouted, "Watch out!"

And someone else, "Keep your fucking gun on him and if he tries to kick me again, shoot him."

And another voice, Eddie this time, and sadly, "My monkey up you tree."

I was standing next to the dining room table and I heard them all coming across the living room: shuffle, shuffle. I wondered what they would think about seeing me with three videotapes in one hand and a shiny strongbox in the other. Would my Ni-Mo uniform offer me protection? I was afraid not. What about my mustache and fake glasses? Nope, again. I have to say that my terror almost got the better of me, but throwing myself down on the floor and wailing wouldn't solve any problems either. There was a door on my left and I opened it. A closet. I entered and shut the door after me, leaving it open a crack. A linen closet. It was not the hideout of my dreams.

Meanwhile, Eddie had been brought into the dining room. Through the crack in the door I could see his white turban. I could also see Steel and Clover. They had eager looks, like hungry men about to eat something greasy. Clover held a pistol. And there was a third man—stocky, black-haired, forty-five, wearing a blue running suit—who I figured was Louie Angel.

"So who the fuck are you?" said Louie Angel. "And if you say anything about that monkey again, Clover's going to shoot you in the knee."

Eddie looked very somber. Slowly he raised his hands and pressed their palms together in front of his chest. "If anyone is despised by others, even if he has committed a serious crime in a former life and been doomed to fall into the evil world, then the sin in the former life is wholly wiped out by virtue of the fact that he is despised in this life." Eddie said this in a high, clipped, anxious voice like he had centipedes in his underarm hair. I have to say I was impressed.

"You gotta hit him," said Steel. Both Steel and Clover were a good eight inches taller than Louie Angel. They looked like pillars on either side of him.

"You hear that?" said Louie, raising his voice as if Eddie were deaf. "Steel says we should hit you."

Eddie lowered his head, "Clay Buddhas cannot pass through water; metal Buddhas cannot pass through a furnace; wooden Buddhas cannot pass through the fire."

"Can I hit him?" said Steel. "Let me be the one to hit him. One pop, that's all I ask."

"Hang on," said Louie. He reached forward and snatched off Eddie's turban. There was a pause, then Steel and Clover began to make hawking noises. Louie dropped the turban on the floor.

Against the spectral whiteness of Eddie's skull were a dozen red splotches. The skull was also knobby and crisscrossed with blue veins. Several of the splotches appeared to be festering but presumably they had been covered with a sort of healing ointment. It made them shine.

"Ugly," said Steel.

Clover agreed. "Really repulsive."

"I thought they were supposed to have hair under these rags," said Louie.

They stared at Eddie, who was staring down at the rug. Louie Angel chewed on his lip. "Something's wrong here." He hurried into the den. There was a sound of furniture being knocked over and the shout, "Son of a bitch!"

Louie came running back into the room. "The case is gone."

At that moment the black maid appeared from the hall to the kitchen. She looked perturbed and perplexed. "Have any of you gentlemen seen that meter man?" she asked.

There followed what might be called a pregnant moment as the three men and Eddie Gillespie stared at the maid.

"Meter man?" said Louie.

"He's disappeared," said the maid. "Either that or he snuck away."

"Son of a bitch," said Louie. "Find him."

Steel and Clover both dashed out of the room. Louie pushed his pistol up under Eddie's chin. "So who the fuck are you?" he asked. With his bald and red-splotched head Eddie reminded me of a baby vulture. He had a depressed look.

"If you going to shoot him," said the maid, perfectly calmly. "I'd appreciate if you'd let me get back into the kitchen first."

She hurried out. From other rooms I could hear doors slamming. I figured I had one minute before I was discovered. As for my fear, it felt like I was getting needles stuck in every square inch of my flesh, as if, psychologically speaking, I was being assaulted by a crazy acupuncturist. It seemed that the very most I could hope for was not to take a dump in my pants. Then I began to hear sirens. They were getting nearer. A few seconds later the sirens seemed to catch Louie's attention and he glanced away. The sirens were right out on the street.

Steel ran back into the dining room. "It's the fucking fire department!"

I could hear large engines and the shouting of men. There was the diminishing moan of sirens that have been switched off.

Other sirens were still approaching. Truck doors were slamming. Staticky voices shouted over two-way radios. A dog was barking. Generators hummed.

Clover appeared from a hallway. "They're coming here," he shouted. "They're dragging their hoses across the lawn!"

"What the hell?" said Louie. "Keep a gun on this guy." He and Clover ran into the living room. There was shouting. A metallic voice said, "Engine fifteen, engine fifteen, please respond." I had a desperate desire to know what was going on. It sounded like the entire fire department was invading Louie Angel's house.

In the dining room, Steel kept his pistol aimed at Eddie, who still had his two hands pressed together in a prayerful attitude. I was afraid that if the firemen saw Eddie's shiny red-splotched head, they would want to shoot water on it. Steel kept glancing nervously toward the living room. As I mentioned he was a big man and he wore a short black T-shirt to go with his short black hair. His big white basketball shoes were still untied. Like his mother should have spoken to him about that. I opened the closet door a little more, thinking I might have to make a run for it.

But that turned out not to be the case, or not exactly. I should say I have never taken Eddie very seriously and seeing him dressed like the Good Humor Man and without his turban and with what I assumed were festering lice bites upon his skull, well, this did not raise him in my regard. But I was wrong. I was doing Eddie an injustice. I had forgotten the other Eddie, the Eddie who had just received his black belt in karate. I mean, you cannot earn a black belt without at least having achieved some expertise. Doesn't that stand to reason? What I mean is the next time that Steel nervously glanced toward the living room, Eddie made a deft movement with his left foot that freed Steel from the burden of his pistol, then he made a flick of his right hand against the side of Steel's head, which seemed to render him comatose, at any rate he fell down. I got to say it was gracefully done.

I jumped out of the closet. "Eddie, let's go!"

At that moment four firemen in black firecoats ran into the dining room and nearly tripped over Clover.

But Eddie and I had had enough. We ran down the hall to the kitchen. There was the black lady holding two dead chickens by their necks, one in each hand. "Did you find the glitch in the system?" she asked.

I paused. "We have found the glitch and it is us," I said. Then we ran out the side door. I figured Eddie wasn't the only fellow who could jive that mystical jive. I still had the three videos and the aluminum strongbox. Although I am not much of a runner, I did very well that day.

We ran across the driveway. Five fire trucks were parked at all angles in front of Louie's house, including a hook and ladder truck. A dozen men were dragging hoses toward the front door. This was very peculiar but I knew it would be a mistake to hang around and ask questions. We ran to the Tercel and climbed in. I turned the key, revved the engine and we were gone.

On the way back to the Northway, Eddie said, "I think I'm being underpaid. I think that was a two-hundred-dollar job."

"It's yours," I said. "I'll make it two fifty."

Then he said, "Would you mind stopping at a sporting goods store, so I can get myself a hat?"

"What team?" I had to say that his bald head seemed to light up the entire car.

"I like the Mets."

"You got it," I said.

"You know, it's good those firemen came running in when they did. Otherwise, I might have hit that guy on the floor when I didn't need to hit him. I mean, hit him just for the fun of it, and that would have fucked up my spiritual equilibrium."

"You got a point," I said.

Eddie rubbed his red-splotched dome. "I wonder where the fire department came from?"

But about that I had no idea.

■ TWELVE ■

I have to tell you that watching a lady slow-dancing with a boa constrictor while she languorously strips the clothes from her delectable body can completely change the way you look at snakes. Even the word "undulation" becomes a new experience. The lady was Sheila Pavic: big, blond and buxom. I don't know who the snake was except that it was a dozen feet long. It would flick its forked tongue against her breasts and flip its tail between Sheila's legs in a way that gave me chills.

Eddie kept shouting toward the kitchen door: "Don't let Angelina in here!" He shouted this over his shoulder and stayed glued to the tube for fear of missing anything.

We were sitting in his living room watching the three video-tapes I had swiped from Louie Angel. All three had Sheila but the snake was different each time: boa constrictor, python and an anaconda. I should think that kind of dancing would take a lot out of a snake. The music consisted of a flute and a little drum, but it wasn't the kind of dancing that required a lot of music. In fact, I hardly noticed the music.

If Sheila fully dressed was a knockout, then Sheila wearing a snake was a nuclear weapon. I began to have some understanding of Joey Weber's infatuation. If you had to make a fool of yourself over a woman, Sheila wasn't a bad choice. Behind Sheila and standing at attention against a white wall were two big black guys in turbans and flowing white robes. I guessed they were meant to be Nubian slaves, but I was struck by how turbans were becoming a motif. They kept their eyes straight ahead as if they had seen Sheila and the snake do this many times before. Ho-hum, they seemed to be saying, Sheila and her serpent once again.

Sure, I had been disappointed not to find the video of me picking up the money in Montreal, but the three Sheila-versus-snake videos made up for a lot. I felt like I had still come out ahead. Unlike *Gone with the Wind* or *Casablanca*, these were videos I would never tire of seeing. And while I had been impressed by my own savoir faire on celluloid (the noble brow etc.), even with a snake I couldn't have competed with Sheila.

"You say, you know this woman?" asked Eddie.

"Only dressed."

"What about the snake?"

"A complete stranger."

We watched all three videos right to the end, which took about two hours. By that time Angelina and Eddie's wife had gotten tired of being penned up in the kitchen. It was only when we had finished that I turned my attention to the strongbox, which was locked.

"I got some tools in the basement," said Eddie. "Let's go check it out."

I had bought him a blue Mets cap, but of course the sides of his head were hairless and his ears looked huge and batlike. At least the red splotches were covered.

At his workbench in the basement, Eddie began to fuss with the case. I had heard of cases that had been wired to explode if foolishly tampered with, so I stood back by the stairs and let Eddie do the tampering. Eddie once spent a couple of years in jail for car theft and during that time he had learned several subversive but useful trades, a knowledge of locks being one of them. And he took a certain pride in it. He could have easily drilled into the case and removed the hinges. Instead, he focused on the lock itself and in five minutes he had it open.

Eddie peered into the box and I looked over his shoulder.

"Ahh," he said, which were sentiments I seconded.

Inside were neat piles of hundred-dollar bills: ten of them. They had a pleasing, shiny aspect, but, like Sheila's boa constrictor, they were a rhetorical device not to be trusted.

"Looks like you can pay me more than two-fifty," said Eddie, patting the money as he might pat his darling Angelina.

I sympathized with him. "It won't work, Eddie. The money's fake. Spend it and you'd go back to the slammer."

Eddie looked sad. "Maybe I could try a simple C-note." There was a plaintive tone to his voice that I understood.

"Hong Kong greenbacks, Eddie. If a bank teller held one of these bills up to a radioactive light, it'd explode. And there you'd be with egg on your face."

But I wasn't really disappointed because the good news was that this was even better than the videotape of me being up in Montreal. By stealing back the actual counterfeit money, I had rescued us from Louie Angel and his muscle. I had committed an act (inadvertently of course) of astonishing genius. I had snuck into the lion's den and come away with his pork chops.

"Shut up the box, Eddie," I said. "I got to take this to Charlie right away."

So by five o'clock I was climbing the stairs to Charlie's second-floor office on Phila Street. In my right hand, I had the strongbox. In my left, I had one of the videotapes. Of the others, one was in my car and the third was with Eddie, who had opined that he wanted to study it a wee bit further.

Charlie was sitting at his desk in his shirtsleeves reading a newspaper. His porkpie hat was perched on his head. Charlie sometimes wore it indoors. He called it "warming his bald spot."

He looked up at me. "Jesse James just got buried for the third time," he said. "Maybe the fourth."

"Sounds like a habit he ought to kick."

"They didn't think it was Jesse in Jesse's grave. They thought maybe he'd never been shot by Bob Ford, that it had been a trick. Some professor wanted to do DNA testing. Did you know that Jesse's great-grandson was a superior court judge in California? His son was a lawyer as well."

"Crime must run in the family," I said.

Charlie gave me a close look. "How come you're wearing a Niagara-Mohawk meter man's uniform?"

"Just another arrow in my quiver."

"Have you been working for them?"

"After a fashion."

This seemed to satisfy Charlie temporarily. "Anyway," he said, "the last time they buried Jesse was in Mount Olivet Cemetery in Kearney, Missouri, after they dug him up from his mother's farm in 1902."

"So was this guy Jesse or wasn't he Jesse?" I asked.

"They seem to think so, but they only found little bits. Then they had some other little bits that they'd been keeping in a Tupperware bowl, fingers and such, that they dug out of his mother's backyard in 1978: stuff they missed when they dug him up in 1902. Now they've added the stuff from the Tupperware bowl to the other bits."

"Does it make up a body?"

"Nope. Just more bits. Actually, his brain was stolen when an autopsy was done back in 1883. Either some doctors wanted to see if they could discover criminal traits or they wanted to sell it. It's probably still in a closet somewhere."

"I'd hate to be buried without my brain."

"But his funeral had a band supplied by the Sons of the Confederacy, a Confederate honor guard, Confederate baton twirlers and the governor made an appearance."

"Sorry I missed it. Maybe they'll have another in a few years. It sounds likes it's becoming a tradition."

"What do you have there?" asked Charlie, nodding toward the strongbox.

"A little surprise," I said, "though nothing compared to Jesse's many bits."

I set the strongbox on Charlie's desk, counted to three and sprung it open. Charlie made a little gasp.

"I was afraid you might get in trouble over that counterfeit money," I said. "So I went and got it back." I saw no point in telling him that getting it was an accident and that Eddie and I would be compost if it were not for the timely intervention of the fire department. "Now you don't have to worry about losing your license. You don't need to thank me. Getting it back was just a simple act of friendship, another good deed in a long chain of good deeds."

Charlie picked up a pack of hundred-dollar bills and riffled through it. Then he looked at a second or a third. I began to get impatient. He seemed to want to look at every single bill.

"There's only one problem," said Charlie.

"What's that?"

"This money isn't counterfeit. Many of the bills aren't in mint condition and the numbers aren't consecutive. This is real money, a quarter of a million bucks of real money."

I was pleased. "Hey, Charlie, it looks like our retirement worries are over."

Charlie glanced at me, then he took off his porkpie hat, looked inside, put it back on and looked at me again. "If Steel and Clover are going to wreck your apartment and wreck your car over a single counterfeit hundred-dollar bill, what do you think they'll do about the theft of a quarter of a million real ones?"

"Maybe they won't know it was me."

"How long do you think it will take them to find out?"

"What if I blamed it on Eddie? He was there too."

Charlie didn't bother to answer. He has old-fashioned ideas about loyalty and honestly that would keep him out of politics and off Wall Street.

"So what do you suggest? Costa Rica for two?"

But Charlie had reached a time of the day when jokes no longer sufficed. Not only did he grimace after I said something, he grimaced when I began to open my mouth.

"We have to return it," said Charlie. "Maybe we can give it to Louie Angel in exchange for the videotape. The main thing is to avoid being killed."

"I also swiped some tapes," I said, tossing the tape onto his desk. "They weren't the right ones. But you'll get a kick out of this. Promise me you'll watch it with Janey at your side. She'll like it as well."

Charlie looked at me suspiciously. "This was one of Louie Angel's tapes?"

"You bet."

I told Charlie some more about my trip down to Colonie with Eddie Gillespie, though again I left out the fire department. I didn't say anything that didn't happen but I didn't say all that did. There seemed no point in having him think me too small of a hero, especially since Charlie had already decided I had made a mess of things. It was hard enough to admit that Eddie Gillespie had disarmed Clover and knocked him out.

"So that's why you're wearing the meter man's uniform?"

"My little disguise."

I was going to tell Charlie that I had a closet full of disguises for special occasions—postal worker, doctor, Santa Claus, undertaker—when the door opened behind me. If there was a knock, I didn't hear it. I turned. It was Joey Weber. He wasn't looking at us, he was looking at the strongbox, which was still lying open on Charlie's desk. Charlie flipped it shut but the gleam in Joey's eye suggested that Charlie had flipped it shut a second too late.

"The heir apparent," I said.

"Shut up," said Joey. He was wearing a brown tweed overcoat that made him look like a brown tweed circus tent. His right arm was in a sling.

"Can I do anything for you?" asked Charlie.

Joey was still staring at the strongbox. "I was going to warn you that some guys stole a quarter of a million from Louie Angel and he's furious about it. He called my old man this afternoon. He thought I should tell you."

"I appreciate that," said Charlie. He slipped a magazine over the strongbox, for which I gave him a C-minus in subtlety.

"A quarter of a million is a lot of money," said Joey.

Somehow I didn't think he was stating the obvious just to be pleasant. I sat half turned around in the visitor's chair to watch him. Joey moved a little closer and the gleam in his eye grew shinier.

"Inflation," I said. "A quarter of a million is just chicken feed these days. People blow that on a weekend in New York. I mean, it's not even worth investing."

"Who do they think stole the money?" asked Charlie.

"A guy in a turban and a guy wearing a Niagara-Mohawk uniform." Joey looked at my uniform. "A uniform like big-mouth's wearing."

"Ha, ha," I said, "this isn't a uniform. It only looks like a uniform."

But Joey was a skeptical cuss. He dug into his pocket with his left hand and withdrew a cute little Italian pistol, the kind with lots of scrollwork on the chrome-plated barrel.

"Pretty," I said. The little pistol in his fat hand looked like a marshmallow lying on a cushion.

"I want the strongbox," said Joey.

"I think you're making a mistake," said Charlie, getting to his feet.

"Sit down," said Joey. "No one's going to kick me this time. If either of you moves, I'll shoot."

The trouble was he was scared. Nervous Nellies pointing guns are far more dangerous then guys like Steel and Clover. With Nervous Nellies you never know if their hands might shake and the guns go off. Believe me, I've seen it happen.

"We need to talk about this," said Charlie. He spoke soothingly, even paternally.

"Shut up."

"You think your dad's going to like what you're doing?" I asked, trying to be calm myself.

"I said, shut up!" Joey thought a little. "Both of you, go to the corner and lie down on the floor."

We did as we were told, though I complained a bit. My body isn't designed to lie on floors. It likes soft beds and hot tubs. Behind me I heard Joey searching through Charlie's desk. I thought he was looking for a gun or even more money, but it was simpler than that. He found Charlie's handcuffs: two pairs. A few minutes later, Charlie was handcuffed to the radiator and I was handcuffed to Charlie.

"This is a dumb idea, Joey," I said.

"What the hell d'you know about love?" he shouted.

It seemed like an odd response, but he followed his question so quickly by giving me a kick in the leg that the oddness of his remark quite passed me by. "Oww," I said. It didn't really hurt, but I saw no point in telling him that.

Joey grabbed up the strongbox. For a fat man he could move pretty quickly. "Next time, I'll shoot you." Then he was gone, leaving the door open behind him. I heard his feet hurrying down the stairs.

"Easy come, easy go," I said. "At least we don't have to give it back to Louie Angel."

"Can you reach the phone?" asked Charlie.

"I can reach the cord."

"Pull it down and give it to me."

I pulled down the phone and it crashed to the floor. Then I dragged it over and gave it to Charlie, who called Eddie Gillespie, who turned out to be having dinner.

"No," said Charlie, "it can't wait. I need you over here right away." He rolled his eyes at the ceiling. "Yes, I realize that you need to spend quality time with Angelina but we need you now." He described our condition, asked him to bring some tools and hung up.

"I wonder what quality time with the darling Angelina consists of?" I asked.

"He said he was feeding her sweet potatoes, you know, all mashed up."

"I thought he might be basting her, you know, for the grill."

It took Eddie about twenty minutes to drive up from Ballston Spa and by the time he arrived I was feeling stiff and bored. Charlie had continued to talk about Jesse James, telling me more about that sociopath than I cared to know. It was Charlie's opinion that if the South had won the war, Jesse would have wound up as governor of Missouri.

"But tell me," I said, "did he brush his teeth, did he help Zelda with the dishes? How was he with his kids?"

When Eddie Gillespie came trotting into the office, once more wearing his turban, I would have considered embracing him, had I not been handcuffed.

"You guys look pretty kinky," he said.

"We're not the ones wearing a turban," I told him.

"See if you can open these, will you?" asked Charlie.

Eddie had brought his little tool case. He was eager. Like karate, picking locks was a skill he rarely got to use. Locks were to him what violins were to Isaac Stern. Within two shakes of a lamb's tail, he had freed us from the handcuffs.

"What'd you do with the keys?" he said.

"You think we did this to ourselves?" I asked.

"Wouldn't surprise me none."

"We had an unpleasant visitor," said Charlie as he rubbed his wrists.

Five minutes later Eddie left snapping a ten-dollar bill Charlie had given him. Fatherhood called, he explained. He had to get back to the darling Angelina.

"Show Charlie those festering open sores on your skull," I said.

"You're crude," said Eddie. He trotted out of the office and I heard him clomp down to the street.

Charlie looked at me speculatively as if not entirely disagreeing with Eddie. Then he went to the safe, opened it and removed his .38. "We've got to find Joey Weber."

In the next couple of hours we went to Joey's apartment, his father's house and a dozen of the bars where he often hung out.

No one had seen him. Personally, I felt that Joey taking the money had relieved us of an unpleasant problem. Now we wouldn't get killed, it would be Joey who got killed. Charlie, however, had a more sympathetic nature.

"Think how his father would feel," he kept saying.

Anyway, around nine o'clock Charlie dropped me off downtown so I could get a bite. He had grown tired of my complaining that I hadn't eaten all day. Afterward, I retrieved the Tercel. I was going to drive home, but as I drove down Broadway, I made an impulsive turn onto Lake Avenue by the police station, which took me out of town on the road to Rosemary's. I didn't mean to visit her. I just wanted to see if she was home and if she was alone. Like I had been torturing myself with torrid scenarios concerning her and Mr. X in the Dodge and I knew I would sleep more soundly if I knew she was innocently alone in her bed. So I drove out Route 29.

The sky had cleared and the moon was a shiny crescent. The rain had melted a lot of the snow along the road but now it was freezing and the road was slippery in places. I tried to tell myself that I was misjudging Rosemary, that the whole thing was a mistake. On the other hand, seeing Sheila naked with the snake had reminded me of Rosemary and I had again thought how Rosemary must have resembled Sheila thirty years ago. I wouldn't say this had made me sentimental but it had brought to mind the passage of time: where we are and what we have and how we got it.

I slowed when I approached the diner, which was shut up tight. Rosemary closes each night at six. There was Rosemary's Crown Victoria parked in front of her little house. There was the Dodge parked right next to it. I rolled down my window and listened. I don't know why. Maybe I expected to hear strangled love cries on the night air. I heard nothing. I considered stopping but I couldn't bring myself to do it. I couldn't trust myself to act like an adult. I drove on a little farther, then made a U-turn and drove back to Saratoga. You may guess that I was feeling a little wobbly on my pins even though I was sitting down. I drove, as they say, in a daze. But then I began to get angry. This guy in the Dodge surely knew about me. He knew he was robbing me of my one and only. He clearly saw me as someone he could toss aside. You see how these thoughts accumulate? By the time I got to town I had worked myself into a rage. A little grocery was still open near the corner of East Avenue. I stopped and bought myself a five-pound bag of sugar. Sweet, sweet. Then I laughed all the way back to the Algonquin.

But my night was not quite over. My apartment was on the top floor. I hurried up the stairs, whistling a happy tune. I came out into the hall and turned right, walked a half a dozen steps, then stopped. My apartment was about twenty feet ahead. The front door was half off its hinges and hanging into the hallway. This would have been terrible enough but there was something even worse. Seated in the doorway was a horrible white animal, small and ratlike but bigger than a rat. It turned toward me and it had a cat's face. Actually, it had Moshe's face. It had Moshe's face and an ugly white body. Then I realized that someone had shaved my cat. When he saw me, Moshe began to yowl in a pissed-off sort of way as if being shaved was my fault. He rubbed against my ankles. I could hardly bring myself to touch him. The skin was nicked a couple of places and had red welts. Moshe looked a lot like Eddie's shaved head.

I took a look inside my apartment. It had been dismantled. Broken sticks that had been my furniture were scattered across the living room. My clothes were scattered as well. I saw macaroni, rice, socks, papers and my electric razor. The devastation of my apartment had easily registered nine points on the Richter scale. I grabbed up Moshe and ran.

■ THIRTEEN ■

After I left Charlie, he meant to go visit old man Weber and feed a little terror into his system. I don't mean with a goblin mask and a Halloween "Boo"; he only meant to tell him what his son Joey was up against and that by swiping the money he was fixing to land on a slab. It seemed to Charlie that several people were on the verge of getting shot. Specifically he was worried about yours truly and Eddie Gillespie, which was a nice quality to have in a friend, but there were others also in danger. I doubt that he was worried about himself. Maybe he's brave, maybe he's unimaginative: who's to say. But if Charlie thought much about himself, he wouldn't be an underpaid private investigator in a podunk town. His main interest was in trying to put the whole mess back together and he felt that the best place to start would be to recover the strongbox, even if it meant returning it to Louie Angel.

But as Charlie was walking down Phila to where his car was

parked, a gray van with tinted windows pulled up next to him and the driver rolled down the window.

"You're wanted inside," said the driver with a growl.

It took Charlie a moment to recognize the man behind the wheel. It was Alphie, George Marotta's nephew.

"Is George in there?" asked Charlie.

"Go look, tough guy," said Alphie.

Charlie considered saying something clever in return, but it was getting late and he was tired and he usually left the witty repartee to me. Instead, he walked to the side of the van. As he reached the door, it slid open. Marotta reached out his hand.

"Charlie, everything's about to go crazy with trouble."

Charlie climbed in and shut the door. Alphie accelerated down Phila, causing Charlie to fall back onto the seat. The top light was on and it was hard to see out the tinted windows. Marotta in his wheelchair sat facing him. One half of his face was smiling, the other had no expression. Next to him was a small refrigerator. "Like a beer?" asked Marotta.

"Sure," said Charlie. "I could do that."

The passing streetlights outside the van made dull orange shapes and Charlie couldn't tell if they were driving down a big street or a small neighborhood street. Marotta gave him a bottle of Heineken and sat looking at him as Charlie took a drink. Now and then Marotta squeezed the small knob in the middle of his nose where the bone had been broken. Because of his stroke it seemed that Marotta had two faces or the same face from different times, or perhaps just a dead face and a living one, because when Marotta talked or laughed one side of his face stayed rigid. Charlie took a second drink and tried to get comfortable.

"Somebody robbed Louie Angel of a quarter of a million this afternoon," said Marotta. "A guy in a turban and a fat, gray-haired meter man. I got no evidence to say it was your friend Victor Plotz but I bet it was."

"Victor's not fat," said Charlie, standing up for me.

"He's getting there."

"Victor thought it was the counterfeit money."

"No such luck. That stuff has already gone down the chute. Does he still have the money?"

"Not really," said Charlie, going suddenly vague. He didn't wish to say that it had been stolen by Joey Weber.

"I don't care where the money is. I just don't want you to think that the theft's the terrible news you might believe. The guys I work for have decided that Louie Angel is getting too big for his shorts and they're nervous about what he'll try next. The thing is, they want to give him away."

"What's that mean?" asked Charlie. He imagined Louie Angel wrapped up in a gift box with a red bow.

"The Feds have an investigation going on. Anyway, my friends feel like sitting back and letting it happen." Marotta gave another little smile with only half his mouth.

"So Louie Angel is about to be arrested."

"Could be. The thing is that Louie is a wary kind of guy. If he thought the Feds were about to pick him up, he'd pull in his legs like a turtle. Consequently, my friends feel it would be best to keep him distracted for a while."

Charlie began to get the point. "And Victor is the distractor."

"Maybe you could help out."

"And what do I get out of this?" asked Charlie. He wondered how ethical it was to receive money from criminals.

"Let's call it a favor."

"I can't eat favors."

"Let me tell you," said Marotta, "in the long run this will pay off. It's good to have friends in low places."

"How long a time are we talking about?"

"A couple of days."

"Will Steel and Clover be arrested too?"

"The whole bunch. But watch out. Louie Angel has got some sense but Steel and Clover like to see how fast they can go. They got no limits."

That was not news that Charlie needed to hear. "Why are your friends so eager to toss Louie Angel to the Feds?"

"The big equilibrium. You got to keep everything nicely

balanced." Marotta paused and lit a cigarette. He blew out a mouthful of smoke, then looked at the filter as if it didn't taste right. "But it's more than that. They're still hoping to see a couple of casinos in Saratoga. A lot of people are against it. If Louie Angel does anything to make the papers, it would hurt the chance of the casinos. People would start shouting about the Mafia and racketeering."

"And Louie is the kind of guy who will make the papers."

"In a big way."

"I don't know how much I can do for you. Help Victor, I guess. Is there anything you can do about Steel and Clover? I'd hate to have Victor get shot."

"Like I say, Louie Angel's a suspicious type. My friends don't want him to know they got their oar in. But if I can do anything, I will."

They finished their beers and their talk drifted off to what various horses were doing and what looked good. Belmont would be reopening in a month.

"I used to go down for the first day," said Marotta, "as regular as a fucking clock. But now all I want to do is sit in the sun."

"You'll be retiring soon?" asked Charlie.

Marotta made a grin that lifted one side of his mouth. "My friends don't think Alphie is ready yet. He still likes girls more than money."

The van dropped off Charlie in front of his office on Phila. The air felt damp and clung to the skin. Small globes of mist encircled the streetlights. It felt like the beginning of a spring thaw.

"The main thing," said Marotta, leaning his head out the door, "is for you to stay alive."

"Thanks," said Charlie. "I'll try to remember that."

The door slid shut and the van accelerated down the street. It was eleven o'clock on a winter night and Saratoga appeared to have drawn its covers up to its chin and be snoring away. Charlie descended the hill to his car.

He wanted to drive out to his cottage on the lake, but he had promised Janey that he would come back to her house: a house that she now referred to as *their* house. However, he was afraid of taking trouble with him. He had big doubts about helping me be a red flag for Louie Angel since the danger could spill over onto Janey and her daughters. At last, he decided to see Janey briefly and explain the situation, then drive out to the lake.

He found Janey at her kitchen table sipping a whiskey, painting her nails blood red and leafing through an old issue of *Newsweek* that had a picture of Princess Diana on the cover. She had come from the hospital an hour earlier and still wore her uniform. She pursed her lips toward Charlie in a kiss and shook the magazine in a companionable way.

"The big lesson to be learned from Princess Di," she said, "is that being rich, famous and beautiful doesn't solve your problems. In fact, it makes your life worse."

"That's what you're supposed to think," said Charlie, pouring himself some whiskey. "It's meant to make you satisfied with the small amount that you have and be happy when you see your wrinkled face in the mirror."

"Do you feel happy when you see your wrinkled face?" asked Janey. "After all, it's not very wrinkled."

"I only feel surprise. I glance in the mirror expecting to see someone about seventeen and I see someone fifty-seven." Charlie took off his porkpie hat and set it on the table, positioning it in the exact center.

"You seem a trifle melancholy tonight."

"I'm not going to stay. There are two guys who might be looking for me and it would be better if you didn't meet them."

"I like all your friends," said Janey.

"These aren't friends."

"Ahhh."

"In fact, they'll be looking for a lot of money that Victor took from them."

"It always surprises me," said Janey in a cheerful voice, "that Victor has reached the seventh decade of his life without being shot."

When this was related to me later, I uttered a little protest. I see myself as likable, kindly, always having a happy smile, a heart-warming sort of guy.

"It hasn't been because people haven't tried," said Charlie.

This was when I arrived lickety-split with my shaved cat and my tale of woe about my wrecked apartment. I knocked at the back door, didn't wait for a happy greeting and pushed my way in.

"Hey," I said. I dropped Moshe on the table. He bared his teeth at Charlie, then jumped onto the floor.

Perhaps I had forgotten how terrible Moshe looked without any fur except a little on the face.

"Yeck!" said Janey.

"Good grief," said Charlie.

Both yanked their feet into the air so that Moshe wouldn't rub against their legs. Moshe yowled, then crouched down by the refrigerator. Not until a cat is shaved do you have a good idea about how scrawny cats generally are. Also, who would have thought their skin would be the same color as skim milk?

"That's Moshe," I said. "He's embarrassed."

"Absolutely humiliated," said Janey.

"What happened?" Charlie asked. He kept his feet in the air even though Moshe made no sign of approaching him.

"Steel and Clover shaved him. You should see what it did to my electric razor."

"Are those the guys who aren't your friends?" asked Janey.

Charlie nodded.

We all looked at bald Moshe crouching by the refrigerator and I'll bet bagels to buttercups that we were all thinking that if Steel and Clover could do this to a mere cat, what would they do to us?

"And they wrecked my apartment," I said. I told them about it. Often I exaggerate but this time I didn't need to. In fact, nothing I said could make it sound bad enough.

"They want the strongbox," said Charlie.

So he proceeded to tell Janey about the strongbox, while I poured myself some whiskey. Then I opened a can of tuna fish for Moshe, but he was too depressed to eat. Earlier in the day, he had been a nice orange cat but now he resembled a crumpled-up disposable diaper. For a cat it had to be a gloomy occasion.

Anyway, Charlie was telling Janey about the exciting events and I was nodding or throwing in a correction or modification when I looked up to the doorway leading into the hall that led to the living room and there were Steel and Clover nodding and grinning at us. Each had an arm draped over the shoulder of the other. Two handsome guys with ugly intentions.

"Jesus," I said, and nearly fell down.

"Front door was unlocked," said Steel with a friendly smile.

"Shows a trusting nature," said Clover. "How stupid."

"Where the fuck would guys like us be without trust?" asked Steel. He raised his eyebrows and waggled his head.

"Jail, most likely," said Clover.

They stood side by side in the doorway: oversized and wearing black T-shirts and black leather jackets. Their short black hair shone in the kitchen light. Steel still hadn't shaved but the stubble seemed neither longer nor shorter, as if the little hairs were applied rather than grown, like makeup.

"Get out of my house," said Janey, standing up. She was about a foot shorter than Steel and Clover and half the width.

"Ho, ho," said Steel. "It's a little late for that."

"Unless you give us the money," said Clover. "Then we'll leave happily."

"See you brought your cat," said Steel. "Little fucker scratched me." He held up his right hand where there was a faint red mark.

"We don't have the money," said Charlie in his honesty-is-the-best-policy voice. "Someone stole it from us." Charlie had remained seated. I had to admire him. He looked perfectly calm but I knew that his insides were doing flip-flops. I wondered if he still had his pistol with him.

Steel and Clover slouched into the kitchen. Their grins lacked amicability. Steel opened a kitchen drawer by the sink, then he opened a second and third. He withdrew a pair of shears. He clicked them together several times. "Now watch carefully," he said. He picked up Charlie's porkpie hat and slowly began to cut it. "Good material," he said. "Nice and thick." He cut the hat in half, then he cut it into quarters. He set the four pieces of the hat back on the table so they looked like a kid's puzzle of a hat.

"First I do that to the hat," said Steel. "Then I do it to you." He grinned and clicked the shears at Charlie.

"That was a good hat," said Charlie, growing indignant.

"Nah," said Clover, "I can't believe anybody liked it. Who the fuck wears a hat like that these days?"

"Jerks," said Steel, "that's who."

"You're better off without it," said Clover.

"You should thank us," said Steel.

Janey had remained standing. She looked frightened but cross. Her face was about the same color as her uniform. "I want you to get out of this house immediately."

"Hey, hey," said Steel, doing a little shimmy. "The lady's got a lip."

"All nurses are lippy," said Clover. "It's part of their job training."

Steel smiled at her. "We want the strongbox," he said. "We get it, then we'll go."

Charlie also got to his feet. I was in my chair, hoping not to be noticed. Moshe was crouched down by the refrigerator. He looked cold without any hair. Someone would have to knit him a sweater. He would need a hot water bottle. And mittens, he needed mittens. Steel and Clover stood in the middle of the kitchen, hands on their hips, legs apart. Steel was chewing gum. Clover kept sucking his teeth. They were both focused on Janey.

"Why don't we shave the broad like we shaved the cat," said Clover.

"I could snip off her hair," said Steel. He clicked the shears. "Too bad her hair's already so short."

That was when Charlie pulled out his pistol from where it was tucked in his belt. Maybe Charlie didn't do it fast enough or maybe he just wasn't sufficiently practiced in such matters, because before he had drawn it level, Steel stepped forward and slapped the gun out of Charlie's hand. It flew across the room, crashed onto the counter by the sink and bounced into a large jar of low-fat mayonnaise, breaking it.

"That was a dumb thing to do," said Steel.

Charlie looked at the broken jar and scratched the back of his head as if to say he would be the last to disagree.

"Where's the strongbox?" said Clover.

"We don't have it," said Charlie.

Steel gave Charlie a push that sent him stumbling back into his chair. "We're not funny guys all the time," he said.

Clover nodded. "Sometimes we're awful guys."

"Sometimes we're absolutely terrible."

"If we don't get that money in about two minutes," said Clover, "we're going to turn this house into complete sawdust."

There followed a tense moment while I wished I was down in Florida walking on the beach. Charlie looked thoughtful. Janey looked furious. I probably looked scared. After all, I had already seen what they had done to my apartment. Moshe slunk across the floor to get behind my legs.

I am sure I had lots of ideas about what was going to happen next. That's what is called probability and studying the options. But instead of any of them happening, there was a high-pitched squeal and from the doorway to the hall Janey's daughter Emma cried out, "That poor cat!"

Well, Steel and Clover were not expecting this. They practically fell over each other turning around.

"Who the fuck are you?" asked Steel, none too politely.

"Don't talk to me like that," said Emma. She was eighteen and very pretty. She had on a flannel nightgown and her feet were bare.

"A morsel," said Clover. "God has given us a morsel."

Emma pushed past Steel and Clover and picked up Moshe and began scratching him under the chin. "You poor thing, you must be freezing." She talked quietly to Moshe and rocked him in her arms. Moshe seemed to like it. At least he never got treated like that when he was home.

"As we were saying," said Steel, staring at Emma.

"We're going to rip this house apart," finished his buddy.

Steel was now holding a pistol, keeping the barrel pointed down at the floor. Clover was watching Emma and the cat. That was the moment when Janey's other two daughters appeared, drawn, presumably, by their sister's scream.

"Oh no!" said the sixteen-year-old.

"Poor kitty!" said the fourteen-year-old. They hurried to their sister as if together they might somehow compensate for Moshe's lack of fur. They too wore flannel nightgowns. All three made much of Moshe, patting him and keeping him warm. I got to say that if I had been the cat, I would have felt compensated. Maybe he purred, I couldn't hear. They ignored Steel and Clover.

"More morsels," said Clover. He didn't say this happily.

"She's probably got a whole football team of morsels," said Steel.

"Who did this to the cat?" asked Emma indignantly. All of the sisters had long brown hair and looked enough alike to be echoes of one another.

"They did," I said, trying to be helpful. "Steel and Clover, they used my electric razor. You think the cat is in bad shape, you should see my razor."

The fourteen-year-old stuck out her lower lip at the two hoods. "You two should be ashamed."

"You should pick on someone your own size," said the sixteen-year-old.

"Hey," said Steel, "we offered to shave your mother."

"Don't you dare," said Emma. "Charlie, make them leave."

I found their trust rather touching.

"Okay, boys, time to clear out," said Charlie.

"Are you fucking kidding us?" said Steel. His unshaven, rumpled face wore a slightly beleaguered look. "You don't seem to understand what we're saying. If we don't get that money, we're doing to dismantle this place and eat these girls for snacks."

But they weren't happy with the girls. They were unknowns

and they threw Steel and Clover out of step, as it were. The girls made them feel they were losing control of the situation.

"You should apologize to the cat," said the fourteen-year-old, crossly. "How would you like it if it happened to you?"

On the counter near the sink were half a dozen ceramic jars containing flour, sugar, salt and some other stuff. There was also a toaster and a blender. Steel reached over and angrily swept them onto the floor. They crashed around our feet, leading us into a rather lively dance step for a moment or two.

"Don't you get it!" shouted Steel.

Emma gave the cat to her younger sister and bent over to pick up the toaster. "You dweebs are awful," she said. Her other sister picked up the blender.

"Poopy," said the sixteen-year-old.

Clover stepped across them and snatched Moshe out of her arms. "You ever seen what happens to a cat in a microwave!"

"Great idea!" said Steel. "Snap, crackle and pop!"

Clover opened the door to the microwave. There followed a tense moment. Moshe waggled his naked feet.

Then the Saratoga fire department arrived.

In the back of my consciousness, I had been aware of sirens, but because of the drama and the crashing and the chance of seeing my dear cat explode in the microwave, I had not paid attention. But now the sirens were right outside the kitchen window and red lights flashed across the kitchen walls. There was a drone as the sirens were cut off one by one. Motors were roaring and men were calling to one another.

"What the fuck," said Steel.

"Not again," said Clover.

Their rumpled faces began to assume gloomy, defeated looks.

By standing on my tiptoes, I could see through the window over the sink. Maybe a dozen firemen were running around in the yard and a bunch of them were dragging hoses toward the back door. Their helmets had red dayglow strips that caught the light. Several carried axes.

"But where's the fire?" asked Emma.

That question probably occurred to all eight of us and the cat as well.

Steel and Clover, however, didn't wait to find out. Clover dropped the cat on the floor and Moshe scampered under the table. Then they ran into the hall and left Janey's house as suddenly as they had come, not even bothering to shut the front door.

"Meanies," said the fourteen-year-old.

■ FOURTEEN ■

A t midnight that same Thursday night, Charlie and I were
buzzing down to Scotia to pay a surprise call on Sheila Pavic.
Charlie was driving his Mazda: whirr, whirr. It had gotten
foggy and the lights of the few approaching cars looked like gray
flowers or the ghosts of cars.

"Maybe she'll show us her snake," I said. "Think what it
would be like to touch what that snake has touched."

"There are other things in the world besides sex," said Charlie, rather sententiously. He was bent over the steering wheel trying to see into the murk. I was trying to think of subjects other
than sex myself, specifically subjects other than the Queen of
Softness and the guy in the Dodge. I kept imagining them in
pretzel-like combinations.

"I suppose you mean money," I said. "Hey, if George Washington had tits my world would be complete."

"I mean things like friendship and love and truth and justice."

"Can't eat them," I said. "Can't touch them, can't spend them, can't fuck them. They're like houseplants. They sit around collecting dust and when people visit they say how nice they look."

"I can't believe you really think that. Think of how upset you were about Moshe."

"It was the ugliness that hurt. I hate an ugly cat."

"I wonder where the fire department came from," said Charlie for about the tenth time.

"They said it was a false alarm."

"But somebody must have placed the call."

"Who?"

"That's what I'd like to know," said Charlie. "Have any ideas?"

"Maybe a nervous citizen."

"And who made the call when the fire department showed up at Louie Angel's?"

"Another nervous citizen. These are anxious times. It used to be that people prayed, now they call the fire department."

"You're satisfied too easily."

"That's not what the Queen of Softness tells me." But, again, at the mere mention of her name, I felt a pang and lapsed into silence. Once past Ballston Spa there weren't many cars. I tried to think of Sheila Pavic and her snakes, then I thought about Steel and Clover and their depredations, but the Queen of Softness and her possible betrayals were like salt thrown in the sugar bowl of my mortal ruminations and they drew my attention from matters of mere life and death.

Charlie had told me about George Marotta and seeing him earlier in the evening. He did not, however, say that we had been retained as unpaid distractions, pseudo-carrots dangling before the mouths of hungry criminal donkeys. Nor did he say, at this point, that the Feds had a positive interest in Louis Angel. He only said that Louie was dangerous, which was like saying the sun was hot.

"Janey's daughters are a brave bunch," I said.

Charlie stared through the windshield into the fog. "They probably had no real idea of the danger. Actually, I thought they'd be mad at me for not being able to protect them better."

"You're kidding."

"I'd liked to have thrown Steel and Clover out of the house. Look what they did to my hat. My head feels cold without it."

"You're well rid of that hat. And, Charlie, we're not young guys. I'd like to prove it all night with the Queen of Softness but I can only make it to about 1:45 A.M."

There are people not born to be crooks and Joey Weber was one of them. He lacked the subtlety required for successful criminality. Joey drove a dark blue five-liter Ford Mustang, a muscle car, and the reason I knew it was Joey's car was that his vanity plate read "JOEY." Crooks should not have vanity plates. It stands to reason. Or if they need vanity plates they should have them with other names than their own. Like Joey's vanity plate should have said "HANK." The Ford Mustang was parked right outside Sheila's apartment house, which was another reason I knew it was Joey's car.

Charlie and I stood on the sidewalk and looked up at Sheila's window on the third floor. The lights were on. Most of the other windows were dark. And the street itself was quiet. People were snoozing, getting ready for the excitement of tomorrow: a Friday with all the charms a Friday brings.

"The trouble is," said Charlie, "Joey has a gun."

"So do you," I said. "Did you get the mayonnaise off it?"

"Most of it."

"I bet you're the only guy in New York State who has a gun that smells like a sandwich."

"Do you have any ideas," said Charlie, ignoring my wit, "how we might take them by surprise?"

"We could go up onto the roof, then use ropes and smash through their windows."

"You've got to stop seeing John Woo movies," said Charlie.

"John Woo shows life as it should be," I said.

But Charlie was already walking toward the front door of the building. I felt he had changed since the destruction of his hat. Without the warming presence of the plaid porkpie, his thoughts had grown cooler and it made him impatient. I hurried after him. The door was locked.

"So how do we get in?" said Charlie.

I pushed a button belonging to a fellow by the name of Robert Sawyer, according to the directory: apartment 2B. I kept pushing it.

"Who is it?" came a sleepy voice.

"Hey, Bob," I said, "I got the money I owe you."

The buzzer buzzed and I pushed open the door. We hurried up the stairs to the third floor on tiptoe, then stopped before the door of Sheila's apartment.

"Now what, wise guy?" asked Charlie.

Charlie didn't realize that getting people to open their doors was as easy as slipping in the tub. When I did a stint as a bill collector, I learned a hundred ways. The trouble, however, was that Sheila's door had a little spy hole. No, not a trouble: a difficulty, a slight hindrance.

I looked around the hall. There were three other apartments and a blank door, which was probably a janitor's closet. I opened the closet. Inside were mops, brooms, boxes of cleaner, an apron and a pile of clean rags. I took off my overcoat, pulled up my pants legs, put on the apron and tied one of the rags around my head. Then I stuffed several other rags down my sweatshirt. Grabbing a mop head, I went back to Sheila's front door. Charlie gave me a look that didn't have a lot of trust behind it.

"Stand to the side of the door," I told him.

I cradled the mop head in my arms so its gray strings were arranged in a neat pile, then I knocked on Sheila's door. "Miss Pavic, my cat is sick," I said in a high voice.

I knocked again. "Miss Pavic, summit is wrong with my cat. It barfs. Miss Pavic, please."

I kept this up. Knock, knock. "Miss Pavic, my cat has got a bellyache. It whoops and whoops."

After another moment, the door opened and Sheila stood before us in her golden glory. She wore a yellow bathrobe and yellow slippers. Her blond hair was piled up on top of her head in a golden beehive.

"Who are you?" she asked, more curious than suspicious.

"Your neighbor," I said. Then I tossed her the mop head. As she jumped forward to catch it, Charlie dodged around her into her apartment.

"Hey," said Sheila.

I grabbed Sheila's arm, pulling her into the hall. "You watch out you don't end up in jail," I said. "You and that snake, you bad girl."

Sheila took a swing at me but I ducked. Then we both hurried into her apartment, where the excitement was already subsiding.

Joey Weber stood with his pistol at his side. He wore green paisley boxer shorts and black socks: that was all. Charlie was pointing his own pistol at Joey's head.

"Drop it," said Charlie.

Joey dropped it.

The strongbox lay open on the floor, surrounded by Sheila's cushions. The rows of hundred-dollar bills shone like fires in the night. I shut the case and tucked it under my arm. It was hard not to stare at Joey's pink belly, which looked like a mutant nougat gone wildly out of control.

Sheila made a grab for the strongbox. "That's mine."

I stepped back. "Don't be silly. It wasn't Joey's to give away."

Sheila was bigger than I was and I was afraid she might tackle me, but she had a healthy respect for Charlie's pistol. By now Charlie was holding Joey's pistol as well. Sheila shimmered and raged in silence. The pillows scattered around on the floor formed a sort of precoital obstacle course. The light had been turned low. I would have given my little finger to see what they had been up to before we arrived.

Joey looked depressed. "I gave her the money. We were going to go away together."

The lovesick doofus. "Maybe she was going to go away," I said, "but I bet she wasn't going to take you."

Joey refused to believe it. Even if he had been a thin guy, he would have been an ugly sucker, with big floppy ears and a nose that hung over his upper lip. You had to feel sorry for him. And if Sheila would pat his hand, scratch his belly and give him a few kisses for a quarter of a million, maybe it was worth it.

"This is Louis Angel's money," Charlie said to Sheila. "You want him mad at you?"

She relaxed a little, then retightened the cord around her bathrobe. One had the sense that she didn't care two hoots about Louie Angel, but she didn't want to make him unhappy. But who knew what she thought? She possessed the kind of beauty that leads the person who has it to think that he or she is the red center of any bull's-eye, the sun around which planets shift, and her true love was an inebriated jockey half her size. Her exterior was one hundred percent perfect, which might lead some poor romantic dreamer like Joey or even myself to imagine the inside was perfect as well. But the inside was only question marks and appetite: the usual mishmash of human uncertainty.

"You're lucky we found you before Steel and Clover did," I said. Sheila curled her lip at me.

Charlie and I moved toward the door.

"Take him with you," said Sheila, jabbing her thumb at Joey. "I don't want him hanging around here any more."

Joey looked crestfallen and he gnawed on his lower lip. I felt sorry for the guy but I couldn't believe that even with all that money Sheila would make him happy. Ladies like Sheila can go through a quarter of a million on a weekend. Joey began to put on his clothes. Both Charlie and I looked away so as not to embarrass him. Joey sat on the floor and tied his shoes. Then he picked up his coat and hat and gloomily followed us out into the hall. Sheila slammed the door after us.

I replaced the apron, various rags and mop head and put on my overcoat. In the pocket I felt a lump. I realized it was the videotape of Sheila dancing with a boa constrictor.

"Don't take it so bad," I said. "I got something to take her place, almost."

"My life is over," said Joey.

Charlie looked sympathetic. He was a romantic type of guy and broken hearts were his stock-in-trade. We went down the stairs, Charlie coming last. He was probably worried that Robert Sawyer in apartment 2B was still sitting up waiting for his money.

Once outside we walked Joey to his muscle car.

"Here," I said, giving him the videotape. "I got this from Louie Angel. He probably had it made."

"What is it?" asked Joey, taking the tape.

"It's hard to explain," I said. "It depends how much you like snakes. But it shows Sheila in all her glory."

As Charlie and I were driving back up Route 52 toward Saratoga, Charlie said, "I wonder what he'll think of the tape. You say Sheila was naked?"

"Well, nobody with a boa constrictor is ever really completely naked. It's probably an aesthetic thing."

It was past one by the time we got back. Charlie put the strongbox in his office safe, a green antique that weighed several tons. Then we drove over to Janey's, where I would sleep on the couch.

Janey had gone to bed and the house was dark.

"Would you like a glass of warm milk?" asked Charlie.

I realized he was serious. "I'll just hit the hay," I said.

He gave me some blankets and pillows and after I brushed my teeth, those old gray tombstones, I got about as cozy as a hot dog in its bun. In two minutes I was trucking into the land of Nod.

Sad to say I didn't stay asleep. Moshe was someplace in the house and he kept yowling. It was a particularly Jewish kind of yowl, a Wailing Wall kind of yowl, a yowl for his lost fur. Baldness, he felt, became him not. As I cranked open my eyes, I found myself wondering if I could do something by sewing several wigs together. Then I thought I could buy half a dozen merkins, but I wasn't sure where I could locate any merkins. I hadn't bought any for a while. Does one look in the yellow pages under pubic hair or toupee? And I wondered how a bald cat would look in a half-dozen merkins of different colors: spiffy or silly? Thinking of merkins led me to think of Rosemary, who had a nice red merkin, two blond ones and a shaggy black one. Then I thought of the guy in the Dodge playing with Rosemary's merkins. By that time I was wide awake and it was only three o'clock.

I got to say that if you spend the wee hours of the night imagining all the raunchy things your typical Dodge owner can do to a woman of Rosemary's beauty and allure, then by the time the sun crests the eastern hills, you will have worked yourself into a rage that would make King Kong's temper tantrums seem like the subtlest mood swings. By six thirty I was in my rented Toyota Tercel and steaming out to Rosemary's diner. It is surprising how fast a Tercel will go if you yell and hammer on the dashboard with your fists. My five-pound bag of sugar was beside me on the seat. Now and then I patted it.

The diner opened at six, so by the time I arrived business had been booming for nearly an hour and there were eight or nine cars in front. But I had no eyes for any old car, I only had eyes for the Dodge. It was parked between the diner and Rosemary's little ranch house. I pulled up beside it, shall we say on the gas cap side of the car. In a jiffy I was standing next to it with my bag of sugar. I won't admit that I poured all five pounds into the gas tank, but I poured as much as I could. Perhaps several tablespoons fell on the ground. I wiped away the stray crystals, replaced the gas cap and put the empty bag in my trunk. Then I blustered my way to the diner with scarcely a diminishment of rage.

Inside was a quiet scene. Rosemary was seated behind the cash register wearing a kind of red satin jumpsuit. Henrietta was serving out bacon and eggs. Old Ernie Boner was flipping flapjacks on the griddle in the small kitchen. About ten folks—farmers, truckers, idle passersby—were chewing placidly. There was the sound of silverware clicking against plates; the hiss of batter from the grill. Then I arrived.

"Who's the guy in the Dodge?" I shouted.

Ten forks paused in midair.

"Vic," said Rosemary, "what's wrong?"

"Who's the guy in the Dodge who's been proving it all night at my expense?"

"What are you talking about?"

"He's in there right now," I shouted, "trying to recover his vital body fluids. Soon as he's awake, he'll want to schtumpf you again. Schtumpf and more schtumpf."

"Vic, there's nobody."

"The hell there isn't." And I slammed out of the diner, heading toward her little house. Behind me I heard the cough-cough of ten erstwhile victual grubbers choking on their chow. I picked up a stone and threw it at Rosemary's front door.

"Come out, you sumbitch!"

I reached her front door and shoved it open just as Rosemary caught up with me.

"Vic, you're making a mistake."

"Ha," I said.

I pushed through the door into the living room. "Where are you?" I shouted.

And there he was, a tousled, oversized, sandy-haired guy in his thirties, still half asleep and getting up off the couch.

"Do I know you?" he asked, his voice blurry with fading dreams.

"Put up your dukes," I said.

He made a vague gesture with his hands and I kicked him in the shin with one of my brogans.

"Yow!"

I got to say that if you are trying to wake a fellow up, kicking him in the shin is an efficient way to do it. One moment Mr. Dodge was sluggishly wiping the sleep from his eyes and in the next he was hopping up and down like the Alexander Graham Bell of the bugaloo.

I got ready to kick him again.

Rosemary shouted: "Vic, no, he's my son! He's my little boy!"

I halted my brogan in midflight, which caused me to execute

a little dance step of my own. The "little boy" was about six feet two inches and easily weighed two hundred and twenty. He looked like a professional linebacker. When I saw how big he was, I thought it had been pretty brave of me to stand up to him.

"I don't believe it," I said.

"A love child of my youth," said Rosemary.

The big guy said, "Hello, Mr. Plotz. Mom's told me a lot about you."

"I didn't want you to know," said Rosemary. "I was ashamed."

There followed a half hour of explanations, much of which I will spare you. The guy's name was Lance Underwood. Lance was short for Lancelot: Rosemary's choice of names back in 1962. Lance was visiting the area and had wanted to spend some quality time with his mom. Normally, he lived in Washington, D.C. He had been raised by Rosemary and lived with her until he was fourteen, when he had gone off to a private school paid for by his father: Mr. Underwood. Looking at young Lance I could see resemblances to Rosemary: the blue eyes, the high cheekbones, the very bigness. Lance stood in front of her, nodding and smiling, then he went off to get dressed.

"Were you really jealous?" asked Rosemary.

"Just a tad," I said.

"I like a man who likes me," said Rosemary. Her red satin jumpsuit shone in the morning sun.

"I'm a man of powerful feelings," I said.

Lance came out of the other room wearing a blue suit and tie. I was struck by how respectable he looked. "I got to get moving," he said. "I'll call you later, Mom. And Mr. Plotz, I hope we get a chance for some conversation. I can't tell you how long I've been looking forward to meeting you."

"Call me Vic," I said.

Lance hurried out to his car.

"What does he do?" I asked.

"I'm not sure. Some kind of government job." Rosemary took my hand and began to stroke it. "Stay with me for a while. The temperature in the hot tub is just right."

Normally this kind of talk would get my body juices flowing, but then my mind registered an unpleasant sound and I turned my attention toward it. It was the sound of an ignition turning over—grind, grind—but not catching. It kept grinding like someone was grinding up pig snouts for sausage. I glanced from the window and I saw Rosemary's little boy seated in the front seat of his Dodge. He wore a frustrated expression. He turned the ignition key again and the Dodge once more took up its note of mechanical complaint. Rosemary was still stroking my hand but it was too late. I was struck down by my realization of wrongdoing. I had maltreated Rosemary's little boy. I had wrecked his car forever. And after that, how could I completely give myself to her sweet embraces?

FIFTEEN

L ance Underwood was scrunched up in the passenger seat of my rented Tercel, shaking his head and scratching his jaw with all the melancholy of an oldster who has been untrue to the dreams of his youth.

"It was a fabulous car," he was saying. "I don't know what could have happened to it. I drove up from Washington just to have it with me. I could easily have flown and rented a car. I've had that car for nine years. It's on its fourth set of tires. You know how some cars have soul? That Dodge has soul. Sometimes when I drive it, I feel like we are one creature, one massive mechanical entity joined together. Its thoughts are my thoughts, my thoughts are its. My very contours, the outlines of my bones, are impressed into the front seat. I could drive it in my sleep. Even now, if I shut my eyes, I can recall the glossy ridges of its steering wheel pressed against my palms. Have you ever felt that way about an automobile, Vic?"

"Nah, drive 'em and leave 'em is my motto," I said. It was, I thought, a necessary lie under the circumstances. I was giving Lance a ride into a car rental office in Saratoga. Sometime in the morning a tow truck would pick up his Dodge and take it to a garage. I wondered what they would find. More importantly, I wondered if they would tell.

"It's great of you to give me a ride," said Lance. "I can't tell you how I've been looking forward to meeting you. What's it been, four or five years that Mom's been talking about you? I had worried about her coming up to Saratoga and being on her own. She's impressionable, you know what I mean? She's all heart and she's easily influenced. She's got the sort of trusting nature that could easily lead her to fall in with the wrong crowd. Men who would take advantage of her. That's why I was so glad when she met a strong person like yourself, someone with honesty and integrity, someone who would do right by her."

I got to say I was about to fling myself into his lap, weep like a banshee and confess, but the Tercel was buzzing along at seventy plus and such a gesture of emotional surrender would have meant the end of us.

"Ah," I said, "I'm not so hot."

"Hey, Vic, you can't fool me. I've been hearing about you for years. I talk to Mom twice a week and every time you're number one on her list of subjects. I'm not a religious man but I've got faith in saints. You're one of the real ones, the kind of guy who'd walk ten miles to help a stranger. Just look how you're giving me this lift. Who knows what kind of important work you're pushing to one side just to help someone you'd never known before today. Mom says that you're a financier. I know what that means, you got to watch the market every second. But here you are giving me a ride. I mean, if there's a heaven, they're watching. They got their eye on you."

By this time I was going seventy-five. I wanted to get Lance out of the car as fast as possible. There was a lump in my throat and a little voice in my ear was urging me to confess. What madness!

"I wish I had known you were Rosemary's kid sooner," I said, which was probably the only true thing I said all morning.

"I can't tell you how I'm looking forward to our good times together," said Lance. "Do you fish? I bet you're fantastic in a trout stream. Already I'm thinking about you as Dad. Do you mind if I sometimes call you that? I mean, in private, just the two of us? You must have had an exciting past. Did you ever do any time as a stock car driver? You really know how to handle this baby. What're you going, eighty-five?"

I got Lance to the rental office in under ten minutes. We shook hands. He had one of those manly grips that plays hell with a person's arthritis. As I drove away, I looked in my rearview mirror and saw him staring after me with a big, goofy grin. He waved until I was out of sight. I drove straight to the Parting Glass and I wasn't myself again until I'd downed two pints of Guinness and four shots of Jack. My hands grew steadier, my heart turned, if not white, then to a lighter shade of gray. Trout streams, I said to myself: fat chance. I hopped into the Tercel and drove to Charlie's office.

But by the time I got there I was once again feeling struck down by guilt. All I could think about was that I had poured five pounds of sugar into the gas tank of a simple-hearted doofus who wanted to call me Dad.

Charlie was seated at his desk with Louie Angel's strongbox lying in front of him. He looked at first as if he was trying to eat the money, then I realized he was copying down the serial numbers. He glanced up at me and nodded.

"I'm evil," I said.

I would have been happier if Charlie had leapt to his feet and said, "Of course not." Instead, he said, "What makes you think so this time?"

"I'm the scum of the earth."

"Has someone been rude to you?"

"I'm serious, I should be shot."

Charlie came to realize that it was no joke. He pushed away the strongbox and looked concerned. On his head he was wearing—I hate to say this—another little hat: not quite a porkpie, not quite a fedora. A sort of plaid hybrid with muted yellow, green and blue squares. Presumably, it warmed his bald spot, but its ugliness seemed the physical equivalent of my woe.

"What happened?" he asked.

So I told him about Rosemary, the mysterious Dodge and Lance Underwood. Then I told him what I had done to the Dodge. Charlie rubbed his chin.

"He thinks I'm a wonderful man," I said.

"Poor guy," said Charlie. He took off his hat, looked into it as if to study its fine interior pinning, then stuck it back on his head.

It didn't seem that Charlie was taking my problem as seriously as he should. I felt as if I had hit my spiritual bottom. By acting on impulse, acting on my emotions, I had caused great harm to someone who should be important to me.

"I tell you," I said again, "someone should put a gun to my head and just pull the trigger."

"Surely you're exaggerating," said Charlie.

"No," I said, "someone should shoot me."

At that moment Petey Loomis staggered into the office holding one of the largest revolvers I had ever seen clutched in a human pair of hands, even though the jockey's were relatively undersized. Its barrel was as long as Petey's forearm.

I scrambled back behind the desk. "I didn't mean it. It was a figure of speech."

"I want the money," said Petey. "It belongs to Sheila."

I don't know if Petey was drunk but he was a long way from sobriety. He swayed back and forth. Five feet tall and under a hundred pounds, it looked like a good wind could blow him away. On the other hand, the .45 was a powerful anchor.

"It belongs to Louie Angel," said Charlie.

"You calling Sheila a liar?" said Petey, raising his voice. Petey was wearing high-heeled cowboy boots, presumably to make him taller, but he hadn't quite got the hang of them and they made him wobble. He clutched the revolver with two hands, holding it straight out in front of him. I could have popped maraschino cherries down the mouth of its barrel.

"He's joking," I said. "We got the greatest respect for Sheila. And her snake," I added.

"Close up the case and give it to me," said Petey.

We did as we were told and in a moment Petey had the case under his arm.

"The trouble is," said Petey, "I got no way to tie you up so it looks like I'll have to shoot you." The prospect didn't seem to trouble him much.

"I've got handcuffs," said Charlie. "You can handcuff us to the radiator."

So in another two minutes Charlie and I were handcuffed exactly as we had been the night before by Joey Weber.

"And if youse guys keep bothering Sheila," said Petey, "I'm going to have to wipe the floor with you."

Then he was gone. Even as I heard his boots clattering on the stairs, I had fished the telephone off the desk and Charlie was once again phoning Eddie Gillespie.

"I hope he doesn't laugh," said Charlie hanging up the phone.

So Eddie showed up fifteen minutes later, turban and all. He was still on sick leave from the city and had driven from Ballston Spa. He gave us a long look.

"Are you guys into something degenerate?"

"We're stuck in an investigative Möbius strip," I said.

Charlie tried to look stoical. "It's great of you to help."

"Maybe you should just throw these handcuffs away," said Eddie.

I demurred. "On the contrary, they saved our life."

"Guess it depends," said Eddie, "on how much a life is worth."

Eddie didn't want to stay and chat. He said he was working hard at home, which I thought must be a crock, but with that, as with other things, I turned out to be mistaken.

Anyway, once Eddie waved his farewells, Charlie said, "Do

you think Petey is taking the money down to Sheila's or is he hitting some bars first?"

"He likes the Golden Grill," I said. "Let's check out a few places."

As we descended the stairs, Charlie said, "How do you like my hat?"

"Where'd you get it?" I asked, not wanting to commit myself right away.

"I found it in my closet." There was a note of pride in his voice as he admitted this, as if his closet was jam-packed with treasures.

"So you could say it's come out of the closet, like they say a gay guy's come out of the closet."

"Sure. I guess you could say that."

"Put it back." By this time we had reached the sidewalk.

"You don't think it suits me?"

"Charlie, you don't want to become the kind of person who a hat like that is going to suit. I mean, if it's a matter of warming your bald spot, even paper towels would be better."

We did a whirlwind tour of a dozen places. The Golden Grill was empty except for a drunk at the bar. The TV was chattering over the cash register. A late winter storm had hit the Midwest, and on the screen were vistas of buried cars and people shoveling snow in Chicago, Detroit and Cleveland. As each city was given its two seconds, the drunk pointed up at the TV saying, "I been there, I been there."

Petey was nowhere to be found.

"It looks like we drive to Scotia," said Charlie. "Just let me stop by the office and get my revolver out of the safe."

So we traipsed back up the stairs to Charlie's office.

"You should keep your revolver with you at all times," I said. "Then you wouldn't get into these fixes like having Petey swipe the money."

"If I'd had my revolver," said Charlie, "Petey would have shot us. Mostly, we're safer without it."

I guess it was because we were in a hurry that we didn't pay attention to the subtleties and cryptic nuances of our environment. Had we been attentive, we might have noticed a slightly different smell, cigarette smoke, aftershave lotion, gun oil. But our minds were too much on the future to pay attention to the present. This was a mistake.

Steel was leaning back in Charlie's chair with his feet on the desk.

"Yo," he said, "the antique gumshoes."

I was in the process of wondering where his buddy was, when Clover appeared behind us and stuck a gun in my ribs. "Tickle, tickle," he said.

"It makes me happy," said Steel, "to see ambition in the elderly. Most old farts your age are toddling off to St. Pete's, but you guys continue to lie and cheat and steal other people's money just like youngsters. It does my heart good to see it."

"Is there something you wanted?" asked Charlie.

Steel beamed. He and Clover had traded in their black T-shirts and black leather jackets for dark brown shiny suits that looked slept in: double-breasted and oversized.

"Our boss wants to invite you for lunch," said Steel.

"We're not hungry," I said.

"That's okay," said Steel, "he's probably not going to give you any food. It's the hour he had in mind, not the event."

"I don't feel like going," I said.

In the next second I found myself lying on the floor on my back. Under my shaggy gray hair a goose egg was taking shape. Clover had smacked me on the head with his revolver. It hurt.

"Don't you see," he said pleasantly, "you got no fucking choice?"

Three minutes later, Charlie and I were at the bottom of the stairs with Clover, while Steel had gone off to get their car. Clover kept prodding me in the belly with his gun.

"I bet if I shot you, you'd explode like a great big water balloon. You'd just go splash."

"This is no way to make friends," I said as I tried to suck in my gut.

"Hey, you had to go mess with stuff that was none of your business. If I shoot you, I'll have no regrets. The world's made up of problem makers and problem solvers. Guess what you are, jerknose?"

I was tempted to formulate the counterargument that Steel, Clover and Louie Angel were the problem makers, but I felt that Clover lacked an objective eye. In any case, the Blazer showed up at that moment and Charlie and I were bundled into the back. Steel took Spring Street around Congress Park, then took Union Avenue out to the Northway. It was still foggy and damp, the kind of weather that makes the baby buds want to burst from the trees in leafy splendor but makes everyone else rather glum. The track looked abandoned and dejected with piles of old snow under the eaves. It was about ten thirty in the morning, which was the time when I usually fix myself a piece of toast with blackberry jam and have another cup of coffee. Not today.

"So," said Steel over his shoulder, "what'd you do with that nice Mercedes?"

"Yeah," said Clover, "we weren't finished with it."

"The nice thing about bashing a Mercedes," said Steel, "is they don't crumple up on you like those Jap cars. A Jap car you bash once or twice and you're done, but a Mercedes you can bash all day."

I looked over at Charlie but he was staring from the window as if his thoughts were someplace in China. Most likely he was thinking about old Bette Davis movies.

"The Mercedes needed an oil change," I said.

"That's inconsiderate," said Steel.

"The Blazer," said Clover, patting the dashboard, "loves to bash. Like the fucking automobile isn't content unless it's making scrap metal. You should get yourself a real car, like this one. Mercedes are passé. Four-wheel drive is where it's at. A real bulldozer."

"Shh," said Steel, "you shouldn't be telling this old fart what he should be doing. He doesn't have much future left. Like if he sees the light of tomorrow, I'll be surprised. He'll be lucky if he makes it to this afternoon. Louie is sick to death of them. So how's the guy going to go out and buy himself a nice car like this one when he should be saying his fucking prayers? His driving days are kaput."

"You got a point," said Clover. "Hey, oldster, you scared of meeting your maker? I hope you got a clean conscience, an old fart like you stealing other people's money and who knows what else, St. Peter will kick your buns to hell."

"That's not how it's done these days," said Steel. "Heaven and hell, they're computerized. St. Peter brings this antique turd up on his celestial monitor and pops the delete key."

With this happy chat we made our way down the Northway to Colonie. But not quite. At one point Clover turned in his seat and looked critically at Charlie.

"That hat," he said, "it's an insult to the human head."

Then he snatched Charlie's hat, rolled down his window and threw it out. Charlie turned in his seat and through the back window he watched his hat bounce along the pavement until it was crushed by a Mayflower moving van.

I t may be surmised that being only five and a half feet tall led Louie Angel into being a tough guy. Look at Napoleon and John Keats, they were both shrimps with a need to succeed. One wondered about Louie's formative years, his childhood on the playground being pushed around by the big kids until finally Louie said, "Hey, I've had enough." So Louie decided to get himself some height. By himself, Louie was five foot six. With Steel and Clover, he was ten feet tall.

Louie was wearing another baby blue leisure suit that matched his baby blue ranch house. He was bouncing lightly on the balls of his feet on his baby blue living room rug and he was popping his right fist gently into his left hand. His talk was not happy talk.

"I want you guys dead so much I can almost taste it." Louie said that and then he smiled and when he smiled you had to realize why the name Anzilotti had been changed to Angel. He looked beatific. Need I say that his eyes were also baby blue.

"I think you're making a mistake," I said. It was pathetic but that was all I could think of saying. That's what fear does to people: it screws up their vocabulary. Steel and Clover were standing slightly behind Louie like a pair of detachable shoulder pads or big leather wings. Charlie was glancing around, not paying much attention, apparently more interested in the decor than the danger.

"My only problem," said Louie, "is in figuring out how to kill you that's long and nasty. Shooting is too simple, drowning is too clean."

"Why not just send us home in a cab?" I suggested.

Louie did something with his lips that was not quite a smile, not quite a sneer. The point seemed to be to show his teeth, which were very white. "Where's my money?" he said.

"Gone," I said.

"What happened to it."

"Someone stole it."

"Who?"

Though I had no fondness for Petey Loomis and Sheila, I didn't care to be responsible for getting them shot. "Beats me. Someone swiped it from the safe during the night."

Louie reached up and gave me a little dope slap on the side of my head. "It's not nice to lie."

"You'll never get the money if you carry on like this," said Charlie, coming awake. "If we had it, we'd give it back. Victor never even meant to steal it. He thought the money was counterfeit money."

"Yeah," I said, "real money, I got no use for it."

Charlie gave me a poke in the ribs. "Victor's concern was the videotape. It still is. If you let us go, we'll get the money and return it to you on condition you give us the videotape. We don't want your money."

Now it was Charlie's time to get a dope slap. Louie reached up and gave him a gentle pop. "Louie Angel doesn't like conditions," said Louie Angel. "You tell me where I can find the money, then maybe we'll talk."

But Charlie didn't like being slapped and he went back to looking out the window, which was hard since the drapes were pulled shut. The muscle along his jaw twitched so at least I knew he was mad.

Louie looked at him for a moment, then shrugged. "Okay," he said, "we're going for a ride." He popped the back of my head in an affable dog pat. "I hear you like Mercedes, how'd you like a ride in a real one?"

I got to admit that a brand-new charcoal gray Mercedes 300E rides a lot better than my gentle antique. Because of the tinted windows and fantastic suspension and glove leather seats it didn't seem as if we were moving at all except when we turned corners. Steel was driving. Clover sat up in front with him. Louie Angel was in the back between me and Charlie. He could stretch out his legs and still not touch the front seat.

"Like a fucking summer breeze," said Louie Angel, "that's how this car drives."

"How's it handle in the snow?" I asked.

"You're jealous," said Louie. "You got the envy written all over your face. That's good, I want you to die unhappy."

"You'll never get the money," said Charlie. "If you kill us, it will be gone."

"Nah," said Louie. "You'll talk. You'll tell me just for the chance to die right away. 'Kill me quick,' you'll say. I know, I seen it happen. You'll be dying to tell. Ha, ha."

"If you frighten me too much," I said, "I'll pee on your nice leather seats."

That kept him quiet for a while.

When the Mercedes stopped I thought we were someplace out of town because there was no noise, but I was wrong. We were down by the river on a piece of predeveloped or postdeveloped land that was just waiting to be turned into an industrial park. Maybe it was in Albany or just north of Albany. Some old warehouses were a hundred yards away. The ground was littered with junk, broken glass, busted pallets, metal barrels. There were five or six big metal shipping containers like the kind they put on trucks, then get carried off by oceangoing freighters. These were rusty and one looked scorched as if someone had tried to burn it. Around it were half-burned two-by-fours and pallets. The brush had been burned away and the dirt looked scorched. It was foggy and the distance was a blur. The other side of the Hudson was invisible; downtown had disappeared.

"Welcome to the oven," said Steel, poking me in the back with his gun. "We could cook bread here if we wanted. As for you"—Steel poked me again—"you're going to be roast pork." His chuckle was like two sandpaper blocks being rubbed together.

"Pizza," said Clover, "we're going to turn you guys into pizza."

Charlie and I were herded around the side of the container.

"The nice thing about this place," said Louie Angel, "is you can scream all you want and only the birds will hear you."

Steel bent over and dragged a broken pallet over to the side of the container. "Too bad the wood's wet. We'll have to get some more from the warehouse."

"That's okay," said Clover. "We need to buy some gasoline anyway. Or is it going to be kerosene this time?"

"Too bad we can't use charcoal," said Steel, "and make it a real cookout."

Charlie and I were pushed around to an opening at the front of the container.

"Step inside, gentlemen," said Louie Angel.

Charlie hesitated and Steel jabbed the barrel of his pistol into Charlie's kidneys. "No turning back now," said Steel happily. "Louie is the Julia Child of culinary catastrophe."

"Yum, yum," said Clover.

Charlie climbed through the opening. I took one last look around. Directly above me I could just see a faint outline of the sun. The fog was clearing and the sun was coming out, which was nice. I followed Charlie into the container. The door clanged shut behind us.

"Put the padlock on it," said Louie outside.

There was a rattling. I gave the door a kick but it stayed shut. The inside of the container was about ninety-five percent dark, the only light coming in through a little rust hole in the top. Charlie took a small flashlight out of his pocket and inspected our new home. Like he is never without a flashlight. I only wished it was a hand grenade. The container was empty except for some charred papers on the floor. Not even a rat was there to keep us company, not even a spider.

"What do you think?" I said.

"I'd rather not," said Charlie.

"Think they'll really start a fire outside?"

"What's to stop them? They'll cook us until we say what we know about the money. Then they'll shoot us."

■ SIXTEEN ■

I have always liked a fire: the happy crackling, the smell of wood smoke. Rosemary has a metal fireplace in her living room and many evenings we have curled up in front of it and watched our lives pass before us in the flames. What is it that the poet said? That in the brightness of the fire one sees all the happy moments of one's life superimposed.

The fire outside of the metal cargo container was not like that, though it did remove the chill from the air. It had taken Steel and Clover about thirty minutes to gather the necessary wood and gasoline but now the fire was burning heartily: happy flames chattering away. Because the sides of the container had grown hot, Charlie and I were seated on the floor in the middle.

"The Chinese have a way of cooking duck that is like this," said Charlie. "The duck is alive and the oven is kept low. Maybe they have plucked the duck. In any case, next to the duck is a container of spicy sauce, which the duck drinks as it becomes increasingly dehydrated. In that way it bastes itself as it dies."

"If they had left us a fifth of whiskey," I said, "we could have done the same thing."

The air was a little smoky but it was more stuffy than smoky. The sides of the container were too hot to touch but the middle was comfortably warm. I began to imagine the point where I had to stand on my tiptoes with my feet blistering beneath me. Then I tried to turn my mind away from the future.

"I'd prefer to have something to read," said Charlie. He sat Indian-style with his legs crossed. His elbows were on his knees. We had both taken off our overcoats. "I've always hated waiting. Shouting does no good, hammering on the door does no good. We can only sit."

"What would you pick for your last book?"

"I don't know, something funny. I've always liked James Thurber. Or maybe *Tom Sawyer*. Nothing depressing."

I tried to imagine Charlie chuckling as he died. "Think of the bright side. Think of the stuff that death gets you out of."

"Like what?"

"Taxes, for instance. Mine are a real mess and April fifteenth is less than a month away. Now I don't have to worry. Or that disaster that Steel and Clover left in my apartment, at least I won't have to pick it up."

"I'll be dying with most of my teeth," said Charlie, perking up a little.

"There, that's the right attitude. And I have most of my hair. No catheters or shit bags hanging from our waists, we're being spared the indignities of old age."

"I miss Janey."

"But think of it this way," I said. "You'll be dying at the peak of your relationship. You'll never have to watch her begin to fall asleep every time you open your mouth to tell her something you find interesting. Best of all, your prick still works, or at least you haven't complained. And look at me, ruining Lance's Dodge, the unofficial stepson I never knew I had. Now I'll never have to apologize. Death means never having to say I'm sorry."

"What about your son in Chicago, your grandchildren?"

"I worry them. Now I won't worry them anymore. Beyond that, I got a little insurance policy. What do I see them, once every two years? Even that was too much for them. I make their hair fall out, even the kids. Now they're about to get a hundred thousand smackers in the mail and maybe another hundred after that. They're going to love me. The kids'll have money for college. My son will be able to finish off the basement. My daughter-in-law will get her teeth fixed. I will be the hero of their happy household. Hey, I should have died long ago." I took out my handkerchief and blew my nose.

"You know," said Charlie, "Janey and I were thinking about getting married. I had a thousand reasons against it. Age, privacy, her kids, money. Now all those reasons seem small and petty."

"There you go," I said. "Count up all the good things you were about to do. Like I was going to give ten grand to the Salvation Army. Whoops, too late now."

"Do you think you would have married Rosemary?"

"I had no plans, but now, what the heck. I'm ready to do it. We can have a double wedding with Janey's daughters as maids of honor, and poor Lance can give his mother away. See all the stuff that death saves you from? Think of it, you'll never catch another cold. You'll never have to floss again."

"I really should have married Janey," said Charlie.

"Nah, you were wedded to your privacy at the lake. Now you can even kiss your privacy good-bye. Your quirks, idiosyncrasies, faults, they'll all be stripped away. Hey, Charlie, you'll be a new man. No wonder dead people become angels. And think of the cops who will be glad to see us go, think of your three cousins and your ex-wife, think of the people you put in jail. Jesus, Charlie, you're about to make a lot of people very happy. Look on the bright side."

I took off my sweatshirt. Charlie was down to his undershirt as well.

"There are people I would have liked to make amends to," said Charlie.

"And now you'll never have to. Fuck 'em."

"Even saying good-bye would have been nice."

"Our funeral will be fantastic," I said. "People laughing and singing. Good-bye, good-bye, you hunk of lard. How they will rejoice. That's my one regret, that I'll miss it."

Charlie started taking off his pants.

"What are you doing?" I asked.

"My long johns," said Charlie, "they're beginning to itch."

"Janey lets you wear those?"

"She doesn't mind."

"I had to agree to let Rosemary buy all my underwear a long time ago. She thinks I look nice in a thong."

"Janey doesn't care what I wear."

Mentioning Rosemary's name made me think of her again: how she looked perched on her stool behind the cash register in her red satin jumpsuit and rhinestones, how she looked floating in her hot tub as a delectable walrus of love, how she looked just sitting beside me and drinking a cup of coffee. And I had to say I missed her. I wished I had her picture in my wallet so I could take a peek at it. It was the one thing I regretted. And I also thought it was too bad I couldn't write her a note, nothing sentimental, just bye-bye and thanks for being my squeeze. I felt a trifle choked up by it, though it might have been the air.

It had gotten smokier, and standing up it was hard to breathe. It was better closer to the floor. It occurred to me that we might die of asphyxiation before Steel and Clover reappeared to ask if we would like to be shot.

Charlie had gone over to the side of the container and was poking it.

"Is the metal soft yet?" I asked.

"It's only warm," said Charlie. "It's not hot anymore." He walked over to the door and rattled it. Then he gave it a kick. It popped open and sunlight streamed in.

"I guess you're going to have to worry about your teeth and hair after all," said Charlie.

"They freed us?"

Charlie bent over and picked up the padlock. It had been cut. "Somebody did," he said, "but I bet it wasn't Steel and Clover." He took a step outside. "And the fire's been put out. Let's get out of here before they come back, unless you're really convinced that death is the right choice."

I jumped to my feet. "I've had a change of heart."

Eddie Gillespie is the kind of guy whose taste in vehicles runs to pickups with glossy purple paint jobs and bright shiny specks imbedded in the paint. Rhinestones again. And around the bottom he had a blue neon tube so that at night the truck seemed to float on a blue cloud. It had lots of chrome, a pair of fog lights, twin spotlights, cream-colored tucked leather seats and four on the floor. But it didn't have a lot of room in the front seat. I sat in the middle. Every time Eddie shifted gears my scrotum clenched.

Eddie called it his machine.

"You're lucky you caught me at home," he said. His white turban bumped the top of the cab. We were on Route 7 heading over toward Schenectady and Scotia. It was past one o'clock and I was beginning to feel peckish.

"I'm really glad you could pick us up," said Charlie.

Since Eddie hated leaving home without his hair, I figured he had only been watching TV. Even wearing his turban in public was an ordeal. People kept asking him to tell their fortunes. The two times he had freed us from the handcuffs he had also made ten bucks telling people about their happy lives ahead.

"I was working," said Eddie, "but I was working at home."

"Got yourself a job licking envelopes?" I asked. "Or are you growing mushrooms in your basement?"

Eddie chuckled in a superior way. "Neither. I've made five hundred bucks just this morning and I owe it all to you, Vic."

I was too surprised to say anything witty.

"You know that tape you gave me of the lady and the snake?" Eddie continued. "I been making copies and selling them for a C-note a shot. You remember the part where she slips the condom over the snake's tail? That's a favorite."

"That was my tape, Eddie," I said. "I stole it. I should get the money." I got to say that I was not happy.

"That's okay," said Eddie, "I was pissed off at you for making me pretend to those hoods that I had a monkey up a tree, but I forgive you."

"You may have the chance to meet that lady very soon," said Charlie.

"It's the snake I want to meet," said Eddie. "I could use it in a swami act."

It was Charlie's plan to go to Sheila's apartment and locate Petey Loomis and the strongbox before the bunch of them took off to Acapulco, Disney World or some other dream spot.

I kept thinking of Petey's oversized .45. I had seen a lot of hardware in the past couple of days and I felt I had reached my limit.

Eddie regaled Charlie with witty Asian chatter. "He who rides the tiger," said Eddie, "must wonder why he climbed on."

The day had gotten warmish and the sun was out. It was one of those days when you realized that winter had shifted to spring. It had been a lousy winter, snow and more snow. Now happy householders were standing in their front yards looking up at the sky with kind regards.

We got to Sheila's apartment house around one thirty. As before, the downstairs door was locked. We stood in the outer lobby looking at one another, then I pushed a few buttons.

We waited.

"Who is it?" came an elderly voice.

"Terminator Exterminators," I said brightly. "Dead bugs is our business."

The door buzzed open and the three of us hurried up to the third floor.

"I don't think that Sheila is going to fall for your sick cat trick again," said Charlie. "And don't forget about Petey's revolver."

"What revolver?" asked the swami. "You didn't say anything about any revolver."

"This is going to take teamwork," I said. "Eddie, give me a cigarette and your matches. Charlie, you stand over there."

Preparations were made.

After another minute, Eddie was lying on the floor puffing cigarette smoke under the door. Charlie hammered on the wall and shouted "Fire!" in a choked voice. I held burning matches under the peephole: somebody looking out would see nothing but flame.

Charlie appeared skeptical but in about two seconds Sheila's door was flung open and Petey came tearing out as if he was doing the Kentucky Derby but without a horse. He held his huge pistol in one hand and the strongbox in the other. We were, as they say, taken by surprise but so was Petey. Eddie was still lying on the floor puffing smoke. Petey tromped on him with his cowboy boots, yelped, and went airborne, flapping the pistol and strongbox like a precursor of the Wright brothers or that Greek kid who wore the wings made out of feathers but messed up. Then Sheila stepped smack in the middle of Eddie's butt.

"Ow!" shouted Eddie.

Petey and Sheila were yelling as well. Charlie was the only one who kept his head. He grabbed Petey and in a jiffy he had both pistol and strongbox. I took hold of Sheila's arm and she smacked me. Then Eddie grabbed her arm and she smacked him too. She was taller and bigger than Eddie. Actually, she looked taller, bigger and blonder than Hulk Hogan.

She stood in her doorway and fumed.

"Eddie," I said, "meet the owner of the snake."

"I don't own the snake, asshole," said Sheila scornfully. "It was a rental."

Charlie began pushing us all back into Sheila's apartment before the hallway filled with curiosity seekers.

"Who's this guy?" asked Petey, jabbing a thumb in Eddie's direction and staring at the turban.

"Way down upon the Swami River . . . ," I intoned.

Sheila started to make a grab for the strongbox but Charlie waggled the .45 at her.

"That's my money," said Sheila. "Petey gave it to me."

"I thought Joey gave it to you," I said.

"They both did," said Sheila. She conceded this with a certain pride.

"But Louie Angel didn't give it to you," said Charlie, "and it's his money."

Sheila pouted. Her blond hair was piled up on her head and she wore a black T-shirt that seemed several sizes too small and black jeans to match. She was like one of those model homes you sometimes see on display: exquisitely finished on the outside, empty on the inside.

"You're going to make me mad," said Petey. "You don't want to make me mad."

He was swaying slightly. He was either half in the bag or half out of the bag, I couldn't be sure.

"What are you going to do?" I said. "Hit me with a swizzle stick?"

Sheila gave me a push. "That's not nice," she said.

"Eddie," said Charlie, "we need your turban."

"No," said Eddie.

"We need to tie them up so we can get out of here."

"No."

"It's for the good of us all," said Charlie.

"No."

So I had to search around the apartment until I found an extension cord. Charlie arranged the cushions on the floor so Petey and Sheila would be comfortable, then he tied their hands together behind their backs.

"I could of killed you before," said Petey, looking up at us from where he lay on his belly, "but I was a nice guy. Next time I'll kill you."

I hoped there wouldn't be a next time.

Two minutes after that we were on our way back to Saratoga. Petey's big revolver was on the floor at Charlie's feet. It was so big that it should have been in the back of the truck. Or maybe we should have rented a U-Haul just for the .45.

"It wasn't very nice of you, Eddie," I said, "to withhold your turban."

"You're not the one with red spots on his head," said Eddie, reasonably.

It was two thirty by the time we got back to Saratoga.

"Now what?" I asked Charlie.

Eddie had parked in front of the Algonquin. I had no wish to go upstairs, where I would be met by nothing but the wreckage of my apartment.

"I want you to go visit Felix Weber and Joey," said Charlie, "and say that we have the money and that we're going to try and return it to Louie Angel around six."

"Are we really going to return the money?" I asked.

"Just do what I ask," said Charlie, slyly.

So I retrieved my rented Toyota and drove over to old man Weber's. Every inch of the way I thought of how my Mercedes was being painted and polished and soon would be as good as new.

I found old man Weber at home. It was his nap time but he confessed to me that he had been unable to sleep.

"It's the anxiety," he said. "It keeps me from breathing regular and being able to drop off."

We were standing in Weber's front hall. He was wearing a purple satin robe: like if he normally took a size small, this was extra large. I could have crowded into his bathrobe with him, had I been so inclined. Poodles were barking in one room; canaries were singing their hearts out in another. It occurred to me that it was for poodles, canaries and his son Joey that Felix Weber was risking his life.

"Has Louie Angel been frightening you again?" I asked.

"He's after me about that money."

"Has he threatened you with death?" I asked.

Weber looked surprised. "How did you know?"

"Charlie has the strongbox," I said. "He wants to return it to Louie around six."

"Counterfeit money?"

"The real McCoy."

"How come he's returning it?" Weber was perking up a little.

"He's tired of Steel and Clover busting up his property."

Weber rubbed his gray little jaw. "A quarter of a million could buy a lot of furniture."

"It's the peace of mind that Charlie values," I said. "And he hopes to get back that video of the Montreal trip."

We chitchatted a little more about the weather and how spring had been a long time coming but I could tell that Weber cared as much about the weather as I cared about the food to be found beneath rocks. His mind was elsewhere.

"So Louie's just going to pick it up?" he asked.

"Something like that."

"At six o'clock?"

"That's the game plan."

I left old man Weber to his cogitations and drove across town to visit his son in his bachelor condominium. After I had hammered on the door for a couple of minutes, Joey opened up. Tears were streaming from his eyes.

"Cooking onions?" I asked.

He stood aside to let me enter. It turned out he was watching the video of Sheila dancing with her snake. Poor guy. It was worse for him than the scene when the hunters shoot Bambi's mother. Sheila had the kind of hips that could rotate three hundred and sixty degrees in one direction while her torso rotated three hundred and sixty degrees in the other. As for her breasts, they seemed to duplicate the entire exercise regimen perfected by the Royal Canadian Air Force. During it all the snake just twisted and twisted. We stood and watched the screen for a moment.

"I love her," said Joey, wiping away the tears on the back of his hand. "I even love the snake."

"You like sad movies?" I asked. "Try Lost Weekend."

"I'll never know anyone else like her," said Joey.

I thought that was probably true, but I also thought it wasn't necessarily anything in her favor. Like he wasn't going to know anyone like the Creature from the Black Lagoon either. Joey stood hunched over in a white T-shirt that looked like he was trying to hide a gigantic water balloon beneath it. You know how some people seem like the human versions of dogs or cats or birds? Joey was like the human version of an eggplant.

"Charlie's got the money from Sheila again," I said conversationally. "He's going to give it back to Louie Angel around six this evening. He wanted you to know. He plans to pick up your markers and get back that videotape as well."

"Six o'clock?"

"That's right, but don't tell anyone."

"Did you see Sheila?"

"Yeah, she was with that jockey friend of hers."

"He's a bad influence," said Joey.

"It's terrible to see a wonderful girl like Sheila dragged through the mud."

While I was carrying out these errands, Charlie returned to his office. He had a number of little plans. For instance, he told me that he was going to take the money out of the strongbox and put it in a safety deposit box in the Adirondack Trust. Then he was going to pack the strongbox with funny money, Monopoly money, copies of the *Daily Saratogian* or *Racing Form*. In that way, the money would remain safe. And he had other plans that I only learned about later, like calling Louie Angel and telling him to bring Steel and Clover. Then, about four o'clock, there was a knocking on his office door and Alphie, George Marotta's nephew, stuck his head around the corner and sneered.

"Unk's downstairs," he said. "Hurry up, I'm double parked."

Charlie talked to Marotta on the curb.

"You know that punishment I told you about?" said Marotta with his head through the window.

"Louie Angel?"

"It's about to occur," said Marotta. "Louie's about to be slam-dunked. Just keep his attention a while longer." Marotta made one of his half-faced smiles.

"He'll be coming up here soon," said Charlie.

"Good, that'll do it."

Marotta started to retreat back into the van but Charlie stopped him.

"I got to thank you for what you did down in Albany," said Charlie.

"What're you talking about?"

"That container by the river."

"What about it?"

"Thanks for letting us out of there."

"You're thanking the wrong party," said Marotta. "I been at the restaurant all day."

"You didn't save our lives?"

"Not today," said Marotta.

"What about the fire department?" asked Charlie. "Did you call them?"

"Why should I call the fire department?"

"Neither time?"

"Charlie, you been sitting out in the sun? What would I do with a fire department?"

"Just wondering," said Charlie.

ometimes when I lie in bed in the morning, and rain, sleet and snow are beating up the atmosphere outside my window, I wonder why it is that I ever drag myself out from under the cozy warmth of my down comforter and tackle the lackluster streets. It is then that I feel grateful for the seven deadly sins. They are lively motivators. Six of them propel us forcefully from bed in pursuit of our boastful concerns, while the seventh, Sloth, sends us back to the sack for reprieve and recuperation so the whole process can begin once again.

Gluttony, Pride, Envy, Sloth, Anger, Lust, Greed—the whole gang gives us reason for living and keeps the indispensable organs humming. Without Gluttony I would waste away to a shadow of my former self. Without Anger my heart wouldn't beat its jungle drums and where would I get the chutzpah to squash the next guy? Without Pride why brush my teeth, wash my face or prepare my corpus maximus to overwhelm the hoi polloi with its beauty?

Without Lust my vigorous manhood would shrink down to less than a dead rutabaga. And doesn't Envy lead us to consider our fellow creatures and not think only about ourselves? As for Greed, it supplies the energy for us to take what they have got. While Sloth, dear Sloth, gives us the chance to rest, recuperate and repeat the whole process ad infinitum, ad astra, ad nauseam.

But it is Greed that is our subject here today: a strongbox packed with a quarter of a million smackers. Who cared who it belonged to? Once we hear that money is floating through the air, don't we feel certain it belongs to us? I deserve it, we say. I need it. I got to have it. And even if we have been struck down by pneumonia and three broken legs, we crawl from our hospital bed and moan, "Mine, it must be mine."

You got to love the human spirit. It never stops till you shoot it. The very fact that Charlie let it be known that he had the money aroused seven people into eager activity: Louie Angel, Steel and Clover, then Petey Loomis and Sheila Pavic, then Joey Weber and his old man. Seven folks for seven sins: Louie Angel could easily be Pride. Joey could play Gluttony on any stage in the nation. Sheila and her snake had Lust down pat. The others were not so clear but Envy, Greed, Anger, they shared them all. Only Sloth seemed short-changed, but maybe I'm wrong. All seven were sinners with gimmicks to beat the system: quick ways to pile up the bucks, knotty methodologies to let them get away with little or no work. Perhaps Sloth drove them as much as Pride or Greed. They wanted the *dinero* so they could put their feet up and never worry about another paycheck. Wasn't Sloth then the foundation upon which their tower of criminality had been built? At least that's how I saw it.

And there was Charlie, sitting at his desk under the large portrait of Jesse James with the shiny metal strongbox smack in the middle of his spotted green blotter. He has a round, angelic face, a little blip of a nose and sky blue eyes that seem to have never looked upon evil, though they have. He knew pretty well what would happen. Indeed, he was the one to suggest to me that we had seven citizens for seven deadly sins.

And who came first? Why, it was Mr. Clover, all by himself in his rumpled brown oversized suit, slipping into Charlie's office about quarter to six.

"Louie sent me," he said.

But Charlie could see the lie. Clover's eyes seemed pinched at the corners and his face had too much fear in it.

"You have a note, of course," said Charlie, with his hands folded on the strongbox.

"A note?"

"Permission from your boss."

"Fuck you," said Clover. He drew a sullen automatic from a shoulder holster and waved it at Charlie. "This is my permission."

"Louie Angel's not going to be happy," said Charlie.

But Clover had no interest in the happiness of others. He jumped forward, grabbed the strongbox and ran for the door, leaving it open. His big feet in their big brogans went clomp clomp down the hall.

Charlie put on his overcoat and followed him, but leisurely. He suspected it would be a long evening.

Clover ran down the hall to the stairs. Just as Charlie reached his anteroom with its ten-year-old copies of *Popular Mechanics*, he heard a gunshot. This was followed by another and another: explosions, ricochets and glass breaking. Then silence. Then a metallic bump, bump, bump, which Charlie soon came to understand was the strongbox bouncing down the stairs. Then a door slammed below.

Charlie hurried down the hall and found Clover sitting on the top step of the stairs with one hand pressed to the side of his face and the index finger of the other poking through a hole in the sleeve of his brown suit coat. Blood was oozing between his fingers, and Clover, Charlie said, had the look of a man who had just hit upon a new philosophy: a meaning of life more pragmatic than visionary. At least his rumpled face expressed a stunned intelligence.

Clover look up at Charlie. "He fucking shot me, the fat fuck."

"Joey?"

"The tub of lard."

"Where're you hit?"

"Look what he did to my ear," said Clover.

He removed his hand and displayed his bloody ear. The top part was missing.

"It must hurt," said Charlie. He removed a clean handkerchief from his pocket and gave it to Clover.

"It must look like shit," said Clover.

"You could say Mike Tyson bit you."

Clover ignored the remark. "And he put a hole in my jacket as well. Look at the cloth. Material like this, it ain't cheap." He pressed Charlie's handkerchief to his ear and it reddened.

"They do a lot of plastic surgery on ears," said Charlie.

Clover sucked his teeth. "I got no health insurance. You can't get it in my racket."

"It must be hard being a tough guy."

"Buster, you don't know the half of it."

Charlie edged past Clover on the landing. "You can use my office if you want. Maybe call a doctor."

"Thanks, I just want to catch my breath. You want your handkerchief back?" Clover held up the bloody handkerchief. Red gouts dripped onto the top step.

"You can keep it."

"Hey," said Clover, "you're a pal."

Charlie hurried down the stairs. It was almost dark and there was no traffic on Phila. A few cars passed up on Broadway. Charlie looked down the hill toward Putnam Street and the Golden Grill. Almost at the corner was Joey Weber. He was probably going top speed but it didn't exceed an expeditious shuffle. Joey was wearing a purple down jacket that accentuated his roundness. On his head he wore a red ski cap with a tassel. In his left hand he held the strongbox. In his right was a pistol.

Charlie started down the hill but just then he saw Sheila Pavic appear from around the corner on Putnam. She didn't have her snake but she was carrying a purse: a thick black plastic rectangle and a gold-colored chain. She wore a tight miniskirt that

Charlie thought must have been cold in the March weather and a short fur jacket that looked like chinchilla but was probably cat. Her blond hair sparkled in the glow from the streetlight. Joey called to her, an eager endearment. Charlie couldn't make out the word but it ended, he thought, in "ums."

Instead of appearing pleased, Sheila hauled off and hit Joey with her purse. Joey's pistol went sailing in the street and slid across the pavement. Reflected light sparkled from the barrel. Sheila snatched the strongbox, then kicked Joey in some place that Charlie couldn't see. Joey sat down with an oomph and Sheila hurriedly crossed Phila toward Spring Street.

When Charlie reached Joey, he was still sitting on the sidewalk with his hands pressed to his groin. His red ski cap with its red tassel was askew.

"You okay?" asked Charlie, touching his shoulder.

"She kicked me."

"Let me help you up," said Charlie.

Joey waved him away. "Never fall in love." Joey's voice was more groan than speech.

"I'll take that under advisement," said Charlie.

"It's worse than any narcotic," said Joey, trying to get comfortable on the edge of the curb. "Even crack is better. I wonder if there's a twelve-step program for women. You know, getting over them. Spiritual progress, not spiritual perfection—all that stuff."

Although interested in Joey's question, Charlie felt he had no time to chat. Up ahead he could see Sheila at the corner of Putnam and Spring Street across from Congress Park. She was walking quickly almost on tiptoe because of her high-heeled shoes. Charlie glanced back up Phila and saw Clover emerging from the stairs to the second floor.

"You just have to say no," said Charlie and he hurried down the street.

Behind him he heard Joey say, "Not only am I powerless over her but she's made my life unmanageable."

Sheila was crossing Spring Street, then Charlie saw her abruptly turn to her right toward the old library. All of a sudden she leapt for the curb, raising one arm to shield herself. Charlie heard the squeal of tires. Hawthorn Spring was on the corner and as Charlie looked past it he saw a yellow Cadillac Eldorado sliding sideways down the hill toward Sheila. Charlie wasn't sure if she screamed or if it was the sound of the squealing tires. The Cadillac smashed up across the curb, knocked down a traffic sign, which said "Slow," and sideswiped a tree in Congress Park. Sheila disappeared behind the Cadillac.

As Charlie trotted down Putnam toward the park, he saw Felix Weber climb out of the Cadillac with his cane, limp around the front end and vanish. Then Weber popped up again behind the hood. His spiky mop of white hair shone like a halo. Weber looked toward Charlie rather guiltily, then hurried into the park, swinging his cane at the bushes. Charlie saw that he clutched the strongbox under his arm.

Charlie hurried across Spring Street and around the front of the Cadillac. Sheila was sitting cross-legged on the grass holding one of her shoes. Her black plastic purse lay in a mud puddle a few feet away. When she saw Charlie, she shook a stiletto heel at him.

"Who's going to pay for this?" she asked. "The heel snapped right off and my panty hose are shot to hell."

"Are you hurt?" asked Charlie.

"I got grass stains on my chinchilla. That old fart tried to kill me."

"He wanted the money," said Charlie.

Sheila glared at him. "Doo dah, doo dah," she said. "Do you always have to say what everybody knows?"

Charlie was going to apologize when he saw Petey Loomis just about to cross Spring Street. Half a block behind Petey was Joey Weber and half a block behind Joey was Clover. Petey was swaying slightly and Charlie guessed that he had been refreshing himself in the Golden Grill.

Sheila saw Petey as well. She got to her feet, holding on to Charlie's shoulder for support as she balanced on one leg. "That old fart took our money," she called to Petey. "He ran into the park."

Petey was holding a small pistol about a tenth the size of the .45 that Charlie had locked in his safe.

Petey came to a halt and stood swaying slightly. In the dim light he looked like a irascible child. "I'll shoot his balls off." Then he glared at Charlie. "What about this guy? Should I pop him?" The pistol, a chrome-plated .22, weaved back and forth in his hand.

"Nah," said Sheila, "he's all right for now."

Petey seemed disappointed. "I guess I better get going," he said. Petey ran into the park, but he didn't seem to be able to run in a straight line and he crashed through a bush.

I wouldn't want you to think that I was snoozing while this was going on. Charlie had told Eddie and me to be out on the street watching the downstairs door on Phila at five thirty and I was ready, I swear I was, but first Eddie had to adjust his turban and then he found a catsup spot on his swami costume and then he needed gas. To tell you the truth, I think he was scared of trouble and he was dragging his feet, but of course he would deny that. But it wouldn't be the first time I had questioned his spunk. Look at these guys who devote their lives to karate, kung fu, judo and tai chi, who pump iron, beef up, pack weapons, learn to throw knives—aren't they motivated only by fear? Maybe Eddie was chicken.

It was exactly quarter of six when he parked up on Broadway: that part of the day that poetical types call the gloaming, a mild day at the end of winter with clouds beginning to move in from the west. A lot of stores were already closed. I climbed out of Eddie's pickup, stretched and looked around. A strip mall sits directly across Broadway from Congress Park: drugstore, pizza parlor, discount doodads, liquor store. Less than fifty years ago it was the site of the greatest hotel in the country: the Grand Union. But the powers of Saratoga felt that a strip mall was more important, so the Grand Union was demolished. Now they are planning to rip down the strip mall and put up another hotel: this is what permits developers and city planners to buy their big automobiles and feel like civic heroes.

Anyway, the strip mall comes with a big parking lot and in the corner right across from the old library was parked a brand-new charcoal gray Mercedes 300E with tinted windows. I was about to remark to Eddie that I had recently ridden in a Mercedes much like that one when its front doors swung open and Steel and Louie Angel popped out like waffles from a toaster. Louie pointed excitedly down Spring Street, then he and Steel began to run toward the park.

I didn't know what he was pointing at, but I was curious. "This way," I said to Eddie.

"Yeah, yeah," said Eddie. Of course he had recognized Steel and Louie Angel and maybe he was dragging his feet.

When we got to the corner, I saw the yellow Cadillac down the hill bumped up on the grass and Joey Weber waddling into the park. What I didn't know was that he had been preceded by a bunch of other people and that the only reason Joey was last was that Joey was slowest.

"Don't you think we should go back to Charlie's office?" said Eddie, once more showing his lack of enterprise.

"You're just afraid of getting shot at," I said.

Eddie stuck out his chin. "Not me, I love bullets."

I felt that his white turban made him a perfect target, but who was I to question his fashion choices. "Let's check out the park first." I began hurrying around the old library.

When the Grand Union Hotel was the glory of Saratoga, Congress Park stood directly across the street, and a pretty picture they must have made. There were great elms in those days and Broadway was lined with them. In the center of the park was the Canfield Casino, a big redbrick building where for many years Mr. Canfield divested visitors of their hard-earned investments at the poker tables and roulette. And there is a pond with a gazebo in the middle and a pond for ducks and a couple of fountains and Congress Spring, since it was the springs that put Saratoga on the map and even George Washington once came to sip and sup. Trees, picnic tables, the whole shebang. Now in late winter the trees were bare, but there were evergreens and shrubbery and of course the general darkness made pursuit a questionable proposition. There were some streetlights around the casino and the major paths were lighted but the rest of it was Surprise, who are you? The park was a maze of bushes and trees into which ten folks had been poured—including yours truly—to grab that strongbox once and for all.

I had barely gotten around the old library when I bumped up against Sheila Pavic trotting along in her stocking feet and holding a dainty pair of high-heeled shoes in one hand, though only one shoe had a heel.

"Hey, hey," I said, "what are you doing here?"

"That old sleazebag stole my money," she said.

"Weber?"

"That's right. Petey's going to shoot him."

And that was the first I knew that the park was full of would-be desperadoes.

"Do you think that's wise?" I asked. "Petey might go to jail."

Sheila gave me a little push in the chest that sent me staggering. "They should never have taken my money and if Petey shoots them, then it's because their karma says they need to be shot. I want my money back. I deserve it." And Sheila disappeared barefooted among the underbrush.

I had to admire her. Never once in the whole business did she consider the money might not be hers. It had been given to her by Joey Weber and again by Petey Loomis and as far as Sheila was concerned Joey and Petey constituted a quorum.

Eddie had disappeared and I was blundering along on my own. Although I occasionally enjoy looking at greenery, I don't like being out in it. It prickles and tries to scratch. Pavement is what I like best: hard surfaces. The trouble with walking on grass is that you can't trust it: gopher holes, quicksand, it's just waiting to trip you up. And if it doesn't trip you or get you muddy, then it's full of stuff that will make you itch or try to nip you. If I want to see a tree, I turn on the Nature Channel. Ahead of me on the other side of some rhododendrons I heard a groaning. A mournful noise. I pushed through the bushes and found old man Weber sitting on the ground rubbing his cactuslike white hair.

"Headache?" I asked.

"That short rascal stole my money," said Weber.

I helped him to his feet and handed him his cane. He wasn't so tall himself.

"Do you mean Petey?" I asked.

"They're lucky I'm not a young man anymore," said Weber. "I'd scrub the streets with them."

"Has it occurred to you that you should go home?" I asked, trying to be helpful. "Maybe take a nap?"

"Then how would I get what's mine? I've worked hard for that money and Louie's trying to cheat me. Even Joey, my own son, is trying to cheat me." What a wonderful facial expression is moral indignation—half astonishment, half concern—like those man/woman creatures once featured in cheap carnivals. Weber shook his baffled head and drifted off among the plant life.

A satellite photo of the park might have shown all ten of us within a few dozen yards of one another, but with the darkness and trees and foliage we might have been in an area as big as Texas.

Eddie Gillespie was hurrying around one corner of the Canfield Casino when he met Petey Loomis hurrying the other way. Petey had the strongbox in one hand and a pistol in the other. Eddie was undeterred, most likely because Petey stank of tequila and beer. If he had run into Steel or Clover, Eddie would probably have wet his pants. In any case, with only a little kick and a chop that he had practiced a scant two million times in his basement rec room, Eddie divested Petey of his pistol and appropriated the strongbox.

"Hey," said Petey.

"Don't get me mad," said Eddie. "I go crazy when I get mad. Then I get lice and my hair falls out."

"You tell fortunes?" asked Petey, rubbing his wrist and staring at Eddie's turban.

Eddie tried to invent a joke that combined the idea of the fortune in the strongbox and the lack of fortune in Petey's future, but it got too confused in his head. "Nah," he said. "I'm too busy."

Eddie continued around the building. He felt a trifle smug. In no time he had rescued the money. Certainly that was worth a bonus. In fact, he didn't see why he shouldn't pay himself the bonus right away from the money he was carrying. Eddie stopped, set the box on the ground and began fiddling with the lock. That was when Steel found him.

"Where's your monkey, swami? Up another tree?"

It is hard to perform a well-executed karate kick when you are crouched on your hands and knees, but before Eddie could even think of it, Steel clunked him in the side of the head with his revolver and Eddie flopped onto his back.

When Eddie again opened his eyes, Steel was facing him with a pistol in one hand and the strongbox in the other.

"You're the guy who kicked me yesterday," said Steel, "and made me look bad in front of the firemen."

"You were pointing a gun at me."

But Steel dismissed the gun issue with a wave of his pistol. "Stand up against that tree, swami."

Eddie did as he was told.

"Guys like you," said Steel, "you're only born to die young. And I got to say I'm glad to be the fellow who's going to settle your hash."

Steel snatched off Eddie's turban and used it to tie Eddie to the tree, going round and round. It was shadowy under the tree and the nearest light was twenty feet away; even so, the red spots on Eddie's scalp shimmered and shone.

"What are you going to do?" asked Eddie, unhappily.

"Think of it this way," said Steel. "I'm going to solve your hair problems."

When Eddie was tied to the tree, Steel began kicking leaves

and dead sticks up around Eddie's feet. Then he took a newspaper out of a trash can and began wadding it up.

"When's your birthday?" asked Steel.

"In May," said Eddie. "Why?"

"Too bad it's not today," said Steel, "because I'm going to turn you into a birthday candle."

Steel took a Zippo lighter from his pocket and began flicking it under the newspaper.

"You're a savage," said Eddie.

"Hey, it's part of my job description."

That was when Charlie put his pistol against Steel's head.

"I don't like killing people," said Charlie. "Untie him."

Steel did as he was told. "Next time," he said to Eddie, "I'm just going to shoot you."

Eddie Gillespie gathered up his turban. "Jesus, Charlie, he was going to fry me."

"I been fucked out of two fires today," complained Steel, "and yesterday I didn't get to cook the cat. I must be losing my touch."

"Tie him with your turban," said Charlie.

"I need to wear it," said Eddie. "I can't leave my head bare."

"You want him running around free?" asked Charlie.

So Eddie began tying Steel to the tree. Charlie grabbed the strongbox and took off through the bushes. Maybe he got twenty feet before Clover stuck out his foot. Charlie went tumbling over it and landed on his back.

"Surprise," said Clover, picking up the strongbox.

Charlie sat up on the ground and rubbed his head. "How's your ear?" he asked Clover.

"It still hurts but the bleeding's stopped." Clover stood over him, a shadow against the greater dark. "Look, I feel bad about this, but I got to shoot you. The boss is pissed at me and if I pop you one, maybe he'll forgive me for trying to steal his money. Sorry about it."

"You mean after I gave you my handkerchief?"

"Yeah, I know. That was your good deed for the day. You sure you don't want the handkerchief back?"

"That's okay. I got others." Charlie had pushed himself up into a squatting position. He was prepared to hurl himself at Clover, but he had no illusions about this. He knew that Clover would only bat him away and shoot him. Still, Charlie preferred doing something active to being shot sitting still.

"I'll try to shoot you in the head so it won't hurt so much," said Clover. "Don't move." He took aim.

"You sure you don't want to rethink this?" asked Charlie, getting ready to jump.

"What the—?" said Clover.

There was a thunk and a groan and Clover fell on top of Charlie.

"Cripes," said Charlie. He scrambled out from under Clover and stood up. As far as he could see, which was about three feet, he and Clover were alone. He could make out trees and the lights of the Canfield Casino off to his left. He looked down at Clover and shone his little light on him. Possibly the man had had an attack. Then Charlie saw a red welt on the back of his head. Charlie asked himself if he should bandage it or administer CPR or artificial respiration, but he was tired of helping Clover so he just grabbed the strongbox, threw Clover's pistol into the bushes and hurried off through the trees.

This time he got thirty feet before someone grabbed him from behind and threw him onto his back. "Oomph."

Charlie looked up and saw Sheila standing over him. From where he lay, she looked about thirty feet tall. She held her shoes in one hand and a pistol in the other. Her purse hung from her shoulder.

"I want my money," she said.

"I told you," said Charlie, "it's Louie Angel's money."

"You lie still," said Sheila, "and I won't shoot you."

Charlie lay still and Sheila took the strongbox.

"You're only making trouble for yourself," said Charlie.

"Honey, that's the story of my life." And Sheila disappeared between the bushes.

All this time I was stumbling around like Diogenes looking

for an honest man and the only difference between us was that he had a lamp and I didn't. I had seen Joey Weber waddle by and I had seen his old man tottering along with his cane. I had seen Louie Angel shouting at his minions Steel and Clover. And I had seen Eddie without his turban, pushing through the bushes with his hands pressed to his dome, whether to protect it or hide it I didn't know.

At the moment I was sitting in a drained pond on the north side of the park. At each end was a statue of an ugly half-dressed guy making a mug at another ugly half-dressed guy crouched at the other end, except since I was sitting in between them, I guess it could be said they were making their faces at me. I had become the focus of their contempt. I was thinking about this when I saw Sheila coming through the bushes on her tiptoes, not very fast because of her tight miniskirt. She was carrying the strongbox. She came straight across the dry pond, looking at one statue, looking at the other statue, then looking at me, crouched down in a similar position and resembling, I guess, a third statue. Anyway, she looked across me and looked away and that was when I tripped her.

"Yeoow."

It hurt me to see her fall, a nice beautiful woman like that. She slid on her belly and her skirt got hiked up to her waist. I snatched the strongbox from her hand and I would have stayed to help, but then I noticed she was gripping a little pistol in among the little grouping formed by her shoes and purse. I sped away as she dropped her shoes and began aiming her pistol.

"You old fart!" she shouted. She shot several times, little crackling noises like wood snapping. I am not much of a runner, bad knees, bad ankles, bad feet, but a few shots aimed in one's direction is a wonderful pick-me-up.

I hurried between the trees and ran smack into Joey Weber and I might have hurt myself were he not so soft. I sat back down on the ground.

Joey stuck his pistol against the tip of my nose. "I'll take that." He snatched the strongbox. "You guys don't get it. I need this money. My whole emotional life depends on it." Then he bumbled away and I tagged along behind.

Maybe Joey had gone ten feet when Steel and Louie Angel appeared on either side of him and each took one of Joey's arms. Were Joey not so big, they might have lifted him.

"Where's the fire, chub?" said Steel.

"Thanks for taking care of my money," said Louie.

"Almost like having it in a bank," said Steel.

Well, Joey gave up. At first I thought that Steel had pushed him, but he just sat down on the ground with a plop. Steel and Louie Angel stumbled on a few feet, then turned around.

"You okay, chub?" asked Steel.

"Depends what you mean," said Joey. "You ever been in love?"

Steel scratched his jaw. "Don't believe I have."

"What's love got to do with it?" asked Louie, heedlessly quoting a Tina Turner song.

"Love still lies ahead of me," said Steel, "at least that's what I figure. Maybe I'm just not ready to settle down yet. I'm still testing the waters."

Louie gave him a poke. "We don't have time for this shit." He clutched the strongbox to his chest and began running up the hill toward Broadway.

By the time I got to the top of the hill, the charcoal gray Mercedes was pulling onto Broadway. Clover was leaning half out the rear window giving the bird to whoever might notice. "Fuck you guys!" he shouted.

Then a green Chevy, about ten years old with a lot of rust, pulled onto Broadway and I saw Petey Loomis sitting on a couple of telephone books behind the steering wheel (maybe he had a cushion). Sheila sat beside him. She seemed to be shouting at him and he seemed to be shouting back. A lovers' spat, I surmised. The Chevy sped after the Mercedes.

Then a dark blue Ford Mustang pulled onto Broadway after the Chevy. I couldn't see who was driving but the vanity plate read "JOEY." It seemed like his hope still sprang eternal.

And after the Mustang came a yellow Cadillac with grass and weeds caught up in its grill and front bumper. Old man Weber glanced in my direction and I waved. He didn't wave back.

It was a regular parade.

At that moment, Eddie Gillespie's shiny pickup with the blue glow strip underneath pulled up beside me.

"Are you just going to stand there gawking?" said Charlie.

There were some sirens coming down Broadway. Somebody had probably reported the gunshots and the cops were toddling over to investigate. I had no wish to talk to them.

I climbed in the pickup and Eddie took off after the Cadillac. He had gone back to wearing his Mets baseball cap. It was subtler than a turban. This time Charlie sat in the middle and every time Eddie shifted his four on the floor, I could feel Charlie clench from top to bottom.

■ EIGHTEEN ■

I did not see what occurred when Louie Angel got back to his baby blue house in Colonie with Steel and Clover, but I had it described to me by several witnesses whose memories were still fresh and throbbing. And I arrived not much later and so I can attest to the accuracy of their description, or at least to the effects of the causes they described. It had begun to drizzle again, a pleasure to the incipient crocuses but no one else. Maybe Louie got home about eight, driving fast and screeching his tires. He parked the Mercedes in the driveway next to the Chevy Blazer, then he ran into his house clutching the strongbox, followed by Steel and Clover. One assumes they felt safe. Possibly they meant to sit down, crack open a bottle of champagne and toast their good fortune. It was not to happen.

Perhaps Louie got a telephone call. Perhaps he noticed some suspicious wires. Perhaps he saw a sparkling fuse. Whatever the case, a piece of unpleasant intelligence was conveyed to him and he and his cohorts exited the house far more quickly than they had entered, their only difficulty being at the front door, where they got briefly jammed together. It was only by fiercely pummeling one another that they broke free and reached the front yard. That was when the house blew up.

One has seen houses: their substance, their dimensionality. They form a significant part of one's life experience. Whether modest or magnificent, they are solid structures meant to protect the occupants from wind, rain, sleet and all those atmospheric conditions that make the mailman's job a hardship. Basically they have a corporeal mass that leads a buyer to plop down cash for their purchase. Would one be so eager to buy if one could be convinced of their intrinsic flimsiness, their physical and metaphysical transience? I ask this because Louie Angel's house was abruptly turned to confetti.

For a moment, the birds in the trees stopped whispering "Louise" and gripped their branches with tiny feet.

Let me itemize a portion of the damage while reminding you that these actions were not sequential but simultaneous.

The baby blue double-sized garage door was torn from its hinges, rose Frisbee-like into the air, spun drunkenly and came down hard on the Mercedes 300E and the Chevy Blazer. This was followed by the garage itself, followed by various garage-type implements: weed chewer, hedge trimmer, lawn mower, snow blower. Glass broke of course, it broke for a block around. The roof of the ranch house separated from the walls and rose upward all in one piece, scattering bits of chimney behind it like rice at a wedding. For a brief period a dozen feet separated the roof from its supporting walls and during those seconds, I was told, tables, chairs, beds, sofas, bureaus, crockery, television sets, the usual odds and ends of domesticity, were seen rising above the walls as if, being deprived of doors, they intended to scramble over the ramparts in the same way that last-ditch hopefuls on the Titanic flung themselves over the railings and into the sea. But there was no opportunity for escape; the roof came crashing down.

It did not, however, come crashing down in one piece. It fragmented, ruptured, smattered and splintered. Perhaps all man-made constructions yearn to return to their natural state: this one did. Sawdust and plaster. Sand and the synthetic polymers and petroleum products inhabiting plastic. And the walls within the house and all the trappings of happy home life were rendered likewise into their constituent scraps, the very screws and nails popped out, seams separated, glue pulverized, wallpaper disjoined and divided itself into postage-stamp-sized units, rugs returned to their threads and the threads unwound. It was not simply a matter of breaking, it was a matter of total disintegration, unqualified attrition.

But once the structure and all its contents were dismantled, then the pieces were shuffled and intermixed as if each article and element had spent its objecthood yearning to be something else: a couch had envied the state of the refrigerator, the furnace fancied becoming a dishwasher, toilets thirsted to be toasters. And suddenly that was permitted them. First they changed places, then in their sundered and whittled condition, they coalesced and intermingled so furnace and dishwasher became one, refrigerator and couch were interlaced like the fingers of a repentant sinner at his prayers.

Then, once these new matchings were complete, it all fell down again to become no more than a hill of rubbish, while above it in the night air rose a cloud of finer debris: the dust kitties from beneath the beds, the tidbits, dabs and minutia tucked in corners, amassed on moldings and collected at the backs of shelves—all were exposed and spread diaphanously across the neighborhood. So the very mites that once occupied Louie Angel's black satin sheets now became the mites of Mr. Jones and Mrs. Kowalski.

Of course there was a noise, first an eruption such as the belch of a gigantic sperm whale, then a rushing and rattling like the noisy roll and flutter of four thousand snare drums as the sundering began and the abbreviated flight of Louie's property was initiated, then a crumbling and banging as once more gravity took hold and the billion bits that had momentarily experienced getaway were returned to the earth not as rain, but rainlike, till at last even the final patter ceased, except for the actual spring drizzle, which continued.

There was no fire.

Louie Angel, Steel and Clover had been proceeding on their bellies toward the street as they shielded their individual heads as best they could. Their clothes in the blast were rent and shredded so utterly that they appeared to have decked themselves out in multicolored ribbons. Then the particles, morsels and scraps that had once been a respectable baby blue house rained down upon them, so they were darkened, chalked up and sullied like lads in a minstrel show preparing to sing Stephen Foster favorites. They had become as dusky and soot-covered as chimney sweeps.

When all was still, Steel raised himself up and looked back at the little hillock that had once been a house.

"Fuck," he said.

He spoke for them all.

Then each stared frantically at the hands of the other two and at the surrounding dirt in a way suggesting dementia if one did not understand the reason for their behavior. For the perception came to all three: the strongbox had been left inside.

It was a sad moment.

They got to their feet.

Though they were bruised and had a variety of little cuts, they thought not of themselves. They moved dreamlike toward the debris, their feet crunching on the particles.

When Petey and Sheila pulled up in Petey's green Chevy, they must have experienced a moment of bewilderment. Steel's Blazer, which now resembled a junkyard relic, had been pulled back and its cracked headlights were sparkling on the stack of scraps that had been a house. In the midst of the rubbish, three murky figures dressed in dark ribbons were digging among the detritus. Theirs was not a casual labor but appeared to a high degree electrified: a sort of hundred-yard dash of digging. Petey and Sheila must have thought they were nuts. Then, once they learned what they were searching for, they joined them.

A few minutes later Joey arrived in his muscle car, followed by old man Weber in his yellow Cadillac.

Then Eddie arrived in his glossy pickup. Charlie and I popped out. By this time quite a few neighbors were standing on the sidewalk observing the show. In fact, I had to elbow my way through the crowd. And there they were, the seven of them energetically digging through this lambasted swelling on the earth, this bump of dust, which only after some reflection did I realize was Louie's former habitation.

The crowd was silent. People knew they were observing something primal. Although Louie, Steel and Clover looked the most peculiar with their spaghetti-ized clothing, the others too had been coated with debris and so were gray from top to toe. The drizzle didn't help.

Charlie and I stood side by side. Various phrases came to mind like "How the mighty have fallen" and "Count no man happy until he is dead," but I held my tongue.

"Gosh," said Eddie.

I would have thought myself incapable of further surprise, but I was wrong. Happening to glance up the street, I saw a man in a gray overcoat and dark suit walking purposefully toward us, followed by several other men similarly dressed.

The man walked directly across the yard, stepping over the litter, toward Louie Angel. His associates followed him. As simply as saying howdy, he withdrew a pair of handcuffs from his coat pocket and attached them to Louie Angel. In a trice, Steel and Clover were handcuffed as well. They seemed too stunned to quarrel with this arrangement. Indeed, their sooty faces even registered relief. Their quest was over, their worries done. They had come to rest in the protective arms of the law.

The man took Louie by the arm and led him back toward the sidewalk. I happened to be standing a few feet away. As he grew closer, he become more familiar. He looked toward me and smiled cordially.

"Treasury Department," he said. "I'm glad to see you're in one piece."

The man in charge was Lance Underwood, the love child of the Queen of Softness, my stepson in sin, as it were. He led Louie down the street toward his rented automobile.

"You know him?" asked Charlie, surprised.

I made a sweeping gesture meant to indicate my general incomprehension. "He's the Queen of Softness's little boy."

The strongbox was not found. Or perhaps, by being pulverized, we all shared in it, but the cash was no longer spendable.

Over the weekend, a vague normalcy was restored. Charlie helped me put my apartment back to order. It was a mess, but I consoled myself with the thought that it wasn't as bad as Louie Angel's mess. Janey's daughters had knit a little sweater for Moshe and he was getting used to it. It was pink. Sheila returned to her snake. Joey Weber returned to his Freihofer cookies. Petey Loomis returned to the Golden Grill. Old man Weber returned to his shekels. But for each, as I shall relate, the thrill was gone.

Presumably the videotape showing yours truly smuggling counterfeit money from Canada to the United States had shared the fate of the strongbox and was returned to its various molecules. In any case, that business was over and done. Real life once more established its grip and spring began its blossoming season. Monday was warm and the sun was shining. Crocuses made their appearance, even the occasional daffodil bobbed its yellow head in warm, protected corners. And the reason for this? It was not simply spring and warmth and blue skies. It was not a seasonal beneficence. All this was because on Monday my Mercedes was returned to me freshly painted and put back to rights. It didn't just resemble a new car, it was a new car. A 1976 honey mustard Mercedes with a purr to put any kitty to shame.

At eight A.M. on the dot I had it in my possession and I took a little tour of Saratoga's glossy streets before tooling out toward Schuylerville to greet the Queen of Softness. But I didn't have much time. At nine o'clock I was scheduled to meet Charlie and Janey at the Spa City Diner for buttery blueberry pancakes and scrambled eggs—all the good things that Rosemary never lets me eat. With Rosemary I would sip a cup of camomile tea, no more, and let her view the Mercedes' fine repainted lines before hurrying to the diner to pack away the cholesterol: pork sausages, biscuits and gravy, bacon and butter and strawberry jam, all the good stuff.

My only worry, hardly even that, was that Rosemary had been a trifle cool to me on the phone.

"Why didn't you tell me that Lance was a cop?" I had asked on Saturday morning.

"Who says he's a cop?"

"I saw him arrest some guys."

"He works for the government."

"He's a treasury agent."

"He doesn't think you like him."

"Why the heck should he think that?"

"That's what he said, that's all."

It was a tepid sort of conversation and over the weekend I had been too busy putting my apartment back together to pay her a visit, even though this played hell with my bodily fluids.

So it was with eagerness that I drove out to her little diner and with dignity and a certain *amour propre* that I meant to reveal to her the Mercedes.

Rosemary was seated behind the cash register in a cream-colored satin jumpsuit looking like a female version of Mount Everest or maybe Kathmandu. We kissed and chatted but all, I felt, was not well. However, I did not have time to investigate. Charlie would be expecting me soon.

"Where's Lance?" I asked.

"Still asleep."

That suited me fine because I had no wish to see him. "Did he get a rental all right?"

"He said it was expensive."

"And his car, what was it, a flat tire?"

"It needs a new engine."

"Ahh. Those American cars."

I finished my tea and we made a date for dinner for the next night. Rosemary sat with her arms folded across her bosom—for her, always a bad sign.

"It would be great if Lance could join us," I said.

"He's got to get back to Washington."

"Damn, I hoped we could become friends."

She gave me a look in which there was an element of doubt. "Next time," she said. Again I had the sense that she was less than excited to see me; that her pulse, if anything, beat more slowly.

I hurried out to the Mercedes. Birds were singing and I knew just how they felt. I turned the key, spun the wheel and headed off toward the Spa City Diner.

Maybe I got a quarter of a mile. The Mercedes made a cough, a sad little noise followed by a whirring rumble that decreased in pitch until the engine stopped. I drifted over to the side of the road. Trucks passed. I turned the key. Grind, grind. I kept turning the key. Nothing. Well, this was a sad state of affairs. I got out of the car and walked back to the gas tank. I flipped open the little lid, freshly painted a fine mustard yellow like all the rest. I licked my finger and touched it to the pipe, then I touched my finger to my tongue. It was as sweet as the memory of romance. Someone had sugarcoated my gas line and my Mercedes had become a shiny hunk of junk.

It occurred to me to rush back to Rosemary's and beat her son to a bloody pulp, but I didn't. As a treasury agent, he probably had a gun. And it seemed that anything I might say, he could easily counter. All my protestations would be in vain. Perhaps you yourself have had the experience of being told that you have brought these events upon yourself. Not only is it not edifying but it lacks charm. Doo dah, doo dah, as Sheila the snake-woman might say.

Instead, I walked to the edge of the road and began trying to hitch a ride to Saratoga. I had an important breakfast to get to with my pal Charlie and Janey, his squeeze. We would start with Bloody Marys and he would tell me the news about old man Weber who had decided to seek retirement and move to St. Pete.

The buying and selling of money had grown too rich for his blood. Then we might have some fried oysters and Charlie would tell me how Joey had bought himself a membership at the YMCA and had joined an aqua-aerobics class. Maybe if he lost a C-note of weight his love life would pick up. Charlie and I would chew our bacon and chuckle. We would pop the yolks of our eggs and dab our biscuits into the bright sunny goo. And he would tell me how Petey Loomis had spent the weekend in the drunk tank of the Saratoga slammer and how Sheila Pavic had decided to move back to Utica where she had roots. She meant to enter community college and become a dietitian. Charlie would say how Louie Angel, Steel and Clover were looking forward to a few years in the federal pen: time to cogitate on their misdeeds and ask if the straight and narrow wasn't the path to follow. We would spoon sugar and real cream into our coffee and Janey would inquire about what had caused the demolishment of Louie Angel's baby blue ranch house.

And so Charlie would tell about George Marotta in his wheelchair and his gloomy restaurant in the hills, how George had engaged Charlie and myself (unknown to me of course) as unpaid coconspirators to keep Louie occupied because some older gangster types guys in snappy fedoras felt that Louie was overreaching himself, felt he had fallen victim to the sin of pride and was digging too deep into pockets where he should not be digging. So they had planned a little surprise party: no drinks, no dancing, but lots of confetti when Louie's house went boom.

And we would chuckle about this as we added butter and gravy to our hash browns and smeared strawberry jam onto our bagels with cream cheese.

And I would say that it was a good thing that Charlie had taken the quarter of a million out of the strongbox on Friday afternoon and stuck it in a safety deposit box, because now we no longer had to worry so much about our incipient old age and how to pay the bills. And I would chuckle about this. But Charlie would grow serious and his brow would cloud. He would speak hesitantly and regretfully. He had changed his mind about the money, he would say. He had been afraid that Louie Angel would open the strongbox and find only newspaper, so Charlie had left the money where he found it, which meant that the quarter of a million had been destroyed after all. And Charlie and I would sigh about that for a moment, then Janey would laugh and shortly we would be laughing too and more Bloody Marys would be ordered.

Then Janey would ask about the fire department and why their trucks had arrived handily on two occasions. Well, I had the answer for that one. Lance had called them. Lance had been keeping an eye on us the entire time and Lance had freed Charlie and me from the oven down by the river and had bopped Clover on the head just when he had been about to shoot Charlie.

"So he was your guardian angel," Janey would say.

But it was more complicated than that and I would think of my Mercedes, which had been turned into a planter, an oversized paperweight, but maybe the fact that Lance had several times saved my life made up for a little.

I thought these happy thoughts as I stood by the side of the road with my thumb outstretched. It was warm but not that warm. Cars whizzed by. Nice ones. BMWs, a Porsche, two Cadillacs, a Continental, a Corvette, even a Mercedes. None stopped. Time continued its unavoidable progression. In the west I saw some clouds moving my way. It would rain later.